EverWar Universe: Avior vs. Dekar a work of fiction. References to real people, events, establishments, organizations, or locales are intended only to provide the sense of authenticity and are use fictitiously. All other characters, all incidents, dialogue are drawn from the author's imagination and are not to be seen as real.

Copyright © 2022. All rights reserved.

Published by Dark Titan Publishing. A division of Dark Titan Entertainment.

Also available in eBook.

Both novellas were originally included in *EverWar Universe: Knights & Lords*.

Paperback ISBN: 979-8-9856344-9-5
eBook ISBN: 978-0-578-29643-2

darktitanentertainment.com

WORKS BY TY'RON W. C. ROBINSON II

BOOKS/SHORT STORIES

DARK TITAN UNIVERSE SAGA

MAIN SERIES
Dark Titan Knights
The Resistance Protocol
Tales of the Scattered
Tales of the Numinous
Day of Octagon
Crossbreed
Heaven's Called
The Oranos Imperative
Underworld
Magicks & Mysticism
The Resistance vs.
Enforcement Order

COLLECTIONS
Dark Titan Omnibus: Volume 1
Dark Titan Omnibus: Volume 2
Dark Titan Omnibus: Volume 3
Dark Titan One-Shot Collection
Dark Titan One-Shot Collection II
Dark Titan Universe Saga Spin-offs Omnibus: Volume 1

SPIN-OFFS
In A Glass of Dawn: The Casebook of Travis Vail
Maveth: Bloodsport
The Curse of The Mutant-Thing
Trail of Vengeance
War of The Thunder Gods
The Trials of Shade & Switchblade

ONE-SHOTS
Maveth, The Death-Bringer
Mystery of The Mutant-Thing
Shade & Switchblade
Retribution of Cain
The Mythologists
Ambush Bot
Kang-Zhu
Cheeseburger Man
Tessa Balthazar
Elite 5
Peacekeeper
Catastrophe Unit
The Nobody Can Beat Up Man

THE HAUNTED CITY SAGA
The Legendary Warslinger: The Haunted City I
Battle of Astolat: A Haunted City Prequel (KOBO Exclusive)
Redemption of the Lost: The Haunted City II
Helper's Hand: A Haunted City One-Shot

SYMBOLUM VENATORES
Symbolum Venatores: The Gabriel Kane Collection
Hod: A Symbolum Venatores Book
Symbolum Venatores: War of The Two Kingdoms
Symbolum Venatores: Elrad's Chronicles
Symbolum Venatores: Twilight of the Gods

EVERWAR UNIVERSE
EverWar Universe: Knights & Lords

PRODIGIOUS WORLDS
Mark Porter of Argoron
Raiders of Vanok
Praxus of Lithonia
The Gods and Men of Argoron

FRIGHTENED! SERIES
Frightened!: The Beginning
Frightened!: The Light Sky

INSTINCTS SERIES
Lost in Shadows: Remastered
Instincts: Point Hope

DARK TITAN'S THE DEAD DAYS
Accounts of The Dead Days

THE HORDE TRILOGY
The Horde
The Dreaded Ones
Our Sealed Fate

OTHER BOOKS
The Book of The Elect
The Extended Age Omnibus
The Eleventh Hour: A Chevah Mythos Story
The Supreme Pursuer: Darkness of the Hunt
Massacre in the Dusk
Venture into Horror: Tales of the Supernatural
The Universe of Realms Omnibus: Book 1
The Universe of Realms Omnibus: Book 2

THE DARK TITAN AUDIO EXPERIENCE PODCAST
Season 1: Introductions
Season 2: In a Glass of Dawn
Season 2.5: Accounts of The Dead Days
Season 3: Battle For Astolat
Season 4: Hallow Sword: Cursed

TY'RON W. C. ROBINSON II

THE STORY OF

BOC	AOC
BATTLE OF CAELUM	AFTER BATTLE OF CAELUM

THE ANCIENT COVENANT
IMPERIUM OF THE DEKAR
CAVALIER CIVIL WAR
WAR OF HELIO

KNIGHT RAYEN AND THE CAVALIER OF LITHIOS - 720 BOC
KNIGHT RAYEN AND THE SEARCH FOR LADY IYERA - 719 BOC
YABEL, THE KNIGHT OF THE SALVATION - 695 BOC
YABEL AND THE LOST GRAIL - 690 BOC
AMRAN, THE PRINCE OF SINSTOR - 675 BOC

RISE OF THE SUPREMACY
ORDER OF THE VIPER

LORDS OF THE VIPER - 435-325 BOC

THE ADVANCED COVENANT

THE ANCIENT KNIGHTS OF ELYON - 325 BOC

ORDER OF THE DAMNED
ZORTH WARS

THE CONQUEST OF SIDHU - 20 BOC
THE DAUGHTERS OF OROS - 20 BOC
NEAR-HUNTED - 16 - BOC

THE INSURGENCY
KNIGHTS OF THE SUPREMACY
ORDER WAR
A DARK MOON
THE JUDGMENT OCCURANCE
THE INTERSTELLUS WAR
HERITAGE

CHAPTERS

- _CONQUERORS_ _____1
- _ORDER REBORN_ _____5
- _OLYMPYA CONQUEST_ _____10
- _BATTLE OF OLYMPYA_ _____16
- _THE DODEKATHEON_ _____19
- _THE COMING HEIRS_ _____23
- _THE CONJUNCTION_ _____25
- _AVIOR VS. DEKAR_ _____27
- _THE GREAT PURGE_ _____30
- _THE LAST ONES_ _____32
- _PREPARE THYSELF_ _____37
- _A YOUNG ABHDI_ _____41
- _AREA 6776_ _____48
- _THE INWARD BEING_ _____61
- _NEGOTIATIONS WITH THE ORCHS_ _____69
- _THE SORCERY PLANET_ _____76
- _THE FINAL PHASE_ _____88
- _BATTLE OF THRAN_ _____98

"IN A TIME LONG PAST, OF AN AGE WITHIN AGES, THERE WAS THE WAR." – THE HIGH ONE

I
CONQUERORS

Sinth Zane and Sinth Sahara, the Lords of the Viper Order, both powerful in the knowledge and power of the Dekar, husband and wife. The two together have made a conquest of traveling through the universe, collecting resources and knowledge that would prove use to them and the Viper Order. Making claim to planets and sectors in the universe at a powerful rate, pouring fear upon those who hate them and despise their philosophy. Now, after taking a claim out of their war against the Herenian Empire, Zane and Sahara have reached their point of climax. Both prepared themselves for their final breaths before entering the realm of the Dekar. Before leaving the realm of the living, they have each handpicked two that will become their successors.

A ceremonial event is held within the Moraltian Castle of the Viper Order. The interior of the castle is filled with a sea of rainshockers, howlsoldiers, Imperial Viper Knights, and residents of Moraltis all standing on opposite sides of the walls as the colors of black, red, and gold consume the environment. In the middle of the floor lays a long and extended red carpet, resembling the dark red of the Viper Lords. Sitting at the end of the carpet are both Zane and Sahara, age had overcome them and their wars of the century has taken its toll on them both. They sat in the seats of the Viper Lords. The front doors of the castle open and two figures enter in, walking atop the dark red carpet. The rainshockers, howlsoldiers, Imperial Viper Knights, and the residents all bow their heads toward the two figures, showing respect and honor to them both.

"Come." Sinth Zane said. "Stand before me and my lady Sahara."

The two figures reached the end of the carpet and stood facing Zane and Sahara. One figure was a man, whom was cloaked in all black with a robe and laced plated armor. A black hood covered his face. The other figure was a woman, dressed in black with a shroud over her face. Both of them bowed and kneeled before Zane and Sahara.

"The time has come." Zane said. "For the change of the air has spoken it and the Dekar allows it."

Zane approached the man and touched his shoulder and he rose up. Sahara approached the woman and touched her on her shoulder and she rose up. Zane reached toward his side and handed the man an aduroblade as did Sahara with the woman. Zane walked over toward a table that stood near the seats. Laying atop the table was the Sinthblade, which is passed down to every Viper Lord throughout the generations. Zane handed the Sinthblade to the man. The man and woman both turned toward each other, looking at one another in the eyes.

"Do the two of you agree to stand side by side in all your works for the glory of the Dekar?"

"We do." The man and woman said.

"Man, do you agree to give the proper orders and instructions to those below your rank and make sure they excel in their works given to them in the glory of the Dekar?"

"I do."

"Woman, do you agree to stand by your husband and obey all that he has to speak toward you and your works?"

"I do."

"Man, do you swear upon the Lord of the Dekar that you will remain faithful to him, to the Viper Order, and to your wife?"

"I do."

"Woman, do you swear to love your husband above all the things within the realm we live in and serve him until your time of calling is at hand?"

"I do."

"The both of you, join arms."

The man and woman joined arms. The man's left arm to the woman's right arm. Within the middle of them stood the Sinthblade, which was in the left hand of the man. Zane commanded them to raise up their arms above them.

"This day, I, Sinth Zane, proclaim the two of you to be henceforth known as Sinth Tyrannus and Sinth Labara. This day, the two of you are crowned as the new Viper Lords of the Order!"

The audience applauded with cheers and yelling. Tyrannus and Labara approached the two seats and place themselves within them, Zane standing next to Tyrannus as did Sahara stand next to Labara. The rainshockers held up their right arms forward, the howlshockers held up their left arms forward, the Viper Knights held up their aduroblades and they all chanted the names of Tyrannus and Labara.

After the ceremony a reception was held within the walls of the Moraltian Castle with residents drinking and partying with each other in celebration of the new crowned Viper Lords. Tyrannus and Labara both attended the party as they sat together at the Viper Lord table with Zane and Sahara sitting with them.

"We chose the both of you for a reason." Zane said. "That being said, we fully believe that the Dekar will truly empower the two of you to do more wonders than we ever could."

"We did our part in the conquering." Sahara said. "Now, it is your turn to do such a task. Make us, the Viper Order, and the Lord of the Dekar proud in all of your deeds in his service."

"Lastly, let the power of the Dekar surge through your being. Let its power show you true knowledge and understanding. With it, the two of you will be able to do and accomplish anything of your heart's desires."

Standing against the walls within the reception are the rainshockers, howlsoldiers, and Viper Knights. Keeping guard of the room and the entrances. Tyrannus and Labara stood up from the Viper Lord table and exited the room. Everyone within the room kneeled down and bowed before them. Chanting their names in the glory of the Dekar. Walking down the corridor, lighted up with fire and the moonlight, Tyrannus and Labara enter their chambers, where their ceremonial bed awaited them as they knew the laws of being crowned Viper Lords. They understood the tasks require for such a position of power.

"I want to see your face." Tyrannus said, removing Labara's shroud from her face and gazing at her beauty, which was shown through her eyes and features.

The two of them both laid down upon the ceremonial bed and desired one another in the ways they pleased. They pleased each other for the entire night, ceasing to run out of energy. That night, Tyrannus and Labara, the new Viper Lords had become one flesh and one in the Dekar.

II
ORDER REBORN

When the sun had risen upon Moraltis, after the ceremonial event of the yesterday, Sinth Zane and Sinth Sahara had gave up the ghost that night and died in their bed. The news had went throughout all of Moraltis and later was caught throughout the universe. Even the Knights of the Abhdi had received word of the deaths of the Viper Lords. All of the nations and planets received the news. Some took is with sadness and grief. Some took the news with joy and celebration. Some received the news with mystery and planning. Their funeral had taken place within the Moraltian Castle and their bodies were placed in a marble-like casket made from the molten grounds of Moraltis and they were laid to rest in the Fields of the Viper, where many of the previous Viper Lords are kept buried.

Sinth Tyrannus sat in the chair of the throne room. His head was hanged low as he mourned the death of his mentor. Sinth Labara sat next to him in her chair, she also grieved the death of her mentor. From the throne room doors entered a lieutenant rainshocker, who approached the mourning Viper Lords.
"Sorry to disturb you, my lords."
"What do you have for us, lieutenant?" Tyrannus said.

"The deaths of our previous Lords have spread throughout the universe. Many of the nations and planets are giving out their reception towards their deaths."

"What of their receptions?" Labara said. "How are the nations handling it?"

"The Sinstorians are grieving, the Abhdi Knights are just, the Ordowians are plotting they've said, the Dagobarians are too busy to respond, and the Herenian Empire is shouting for joy and having a celebration."

"The Elladians." Tyrannus said. "Them!"

"What of the Elladians, beloved?"

"They're responsible for our mentors' deaths. Their planet of Ellada was our mentors' last attempt at conquering a planet for our Order. They failed in the task due to interference from the Abhdi Knights and their prized warrior called Serkelrod."

"We appreciate the news, lieutenant. You may leave us."

"Yes, my lords." The lieutenant said, leaving the throne room.

Tyrannus stood up from the chair and walked towards the window behind them, he gazed out towards the fields of Moraltis, witnessing those walking through its green and yellow grounds as well as gazing at the graves of those who came before him and his rule. Labara slowly approached him, hugging him from behind.

"What are you plotting out?"

"Our mentors failed in conquering Ellada from the Herenian Empire. I say, we should finish what they started. Let us lead our armies to Ellada and conquer their planet and claim everything there our own. What of a better way to make our mentors and our Lord proud."

"I am with you with whatever you desire, beloved. But, how will we handle the possible interference of the Abhdi Knights or the Cavaliers?"

"They have yet to feel our power, my love. The Dekar flows through us much more than our mentors. With its power in our hands, we can wipe out the Knights of the Covenant and the Emerald Cavaliers from the universe. Make it clean once more."

"I love when you speak in such a manner."

"First, we'll have to rally up our soldiers. Prepare them for the journey. Meanwhile, you and I will have to acquire a hunter to our advantage."

"Anyone you had in mind, beloved?"

"There is a man whom I've heard about that scouts the universe. Hunt after hunt he roams and receives his rewards in completing his missions. His name is Jakah Pen, the universe's best bounty hunter. So he is called."

"I will get right onto it."

Labara exited the throne room while Tyrannus walked away from the window and near a shrine that was built within the throne room. The shrine is a marble-like statue of their Lord, the one whom is said to have spread the Dekar through the universe. The statue had remnants of what their Lord happened to look like. From his great physique to his wings and to his features. The statue stood tall in the face of Tyrannus, who bowed down before it. His head bowed as well.

"My Lord, my Master, my Mighty One, we will need your guidance and strength for the tasks that stand before us. Show me the power as you've shown my mentor and my fathers before me. Show me and my wife the power of the Dekar. The power that you spread across the universe for those who wish to possess it. We wish to make you proud and to exalt you above our own selves. For we are nothing but fleshly beings walking amidst a planet that the first enash never touched. We were made of the ground, but you were made of the fire. Please, I ask of you, give us an inch of that fire you were created and formed in. give us that fire and through it, the Dekar will be evermore stronger and powerful than it was before."

Tyrannus stood up and walked from the statue, also leaving

the throne room. A low humming sound was coming from the statue, as if something was embedded within its marble feature.

Labara had made the call and from the skies of Moraltis, came down a ship. The ship was silver and blue, almost the shape of a rectangle, but with an end similar to a circle. The ship made its landing and walking out of its hangar doors was Jakah Pen, covered in his light gray armor and his face hidden within his light gray and blue helmet. Jakah was guided by two rainshockers, who lead him toward the throne room. Approaching the room, the two hooded guards opened the door for Jakah to enter, as he entered, he could see Tyrannus and Labara sitting down in the chairs, facing him.

"You've called to see me, Viper Lords?" Jakah said with a muffled voice.

"It is of a very importance." Tyrannus said.

Jakah walked toward them and kneeled before them. Showing his respect and honor. He arose and faced the newly Viper Lords. Tyrannus and Labara measured Jakah from his stance and the weapons that were placed around his armored body.

"You surely come prepared." Labara said.

"I am always prepared for a mission. What mission do you have of me to proceed?"

"We will need you to assist us in invading the planet of Ellada. The home of the Herenian Empire. We seek to wipe them out completely and claim their home as one of our own."

"You seek to eliminate the Elladians from the universe? I like the mission already."

"Though, there is a catch to this mission of ours."

"What catch?"

"The invasion will be in several years time."

"How many years are you talking?"

"An estimated amount of thirty-five years."

"Thirty-five years until you invade? That's your mission?"

"There is a prime reason for the time span of our mission.

Our rainshockers aren't fully prepared for the might of their female warriors and their Princess. They need proper training and I was hoping you would give it to them."

"You're giving me the opportunity of training rainshockers. Plus invading Ellada?"

"That is what we're offering to you, Jakah. So, what will be your answer?"

"My answer is simple. I'm in. just, what will I be rewarded with, if I may ask of it."

"The spoils of victory. Whatever your eyes look upon and desire shall be yours to have."

"Anything my eyes lust after will be mine to have. That's what you're telling me?"

"It is. Whatever you so desire."

"I am honored of this, Viper Lords. I will train your rainshockers and turn them into primary soldiers with heightened skills. They'll be different than any other armies you may have seen in your young lifetime. When the time comes, I will assist you in conquering Ellada and putting an end to their Herenian Empire."

Jakah bowed and left the throne room. Tyrannus turned to Labara with a smile on his face as he pulled back his black hood from over his face.

"Our plan is going as we hoped it would." Tyrannus said. "Jakah will train our shockers and when the thirty-five year line ends, we will invade their world and destroy them from the universe."

"And what of the Knights or the Cavaliers?"

"They will feel the might of our rainshockers, Jakah's abilities, and our power of the Dekar."

They kissed one another before leaving the throne room and entering their chambers to revel in their love with one another.

III

OLYMPYA CONQUEST
400 YEARS DURING THE BATTLE OF CAELUM

The thirty-five years have passed since the agreement was made between the Viper Lords and Jakah Pen concerning the invasion of Ellada. Jakah stayed on Moraltis and trained the thousands of rainshockers and even the howlsoldiers that attended the training sessions. He taught them the arts of hunting, fighting, swordsmanship, hand-to-hand combat, amongst other feats fit for warfare. Tyrannus and Labara spoke with their council detaining the route to Ellada and the easiest way to enter the planet without being spotted by the watchers of the air.

"How are we able to reach Ellada without being spotted in their skies?" said a member of the Council.

"We shouldn't have to worry about them noticing us before we land." Tyrannus said. "They will see us when we land."

"Are you sure that's an intelligent plan, my lord?"

"It is when I have spoken it."

The Council members turned to each other. Their eyes and facial expressions showing the possibility of fear in their spirits as they look at Tyrannus and Labara. They bow before them, leaving the council room.

"Send word out to Jakah." Tyrannus said. "Tell him to rally up the rainshockers for Ellada."

"I will do so, beloved."

Outside of the castle, Labara approached Jakah, as he stood with the rainshockers and howlshockers. Jakah nodded before Labara. She gazed out at the rainshockers and turned toward the howlshockers. She smiled as she faced Jakah.

"I can sense they are ready for the battle ahead."

"They have been trained to the highest possibilities, your highness." Jakah said. "I see that you have some news to tell me? Are we preparing to head out toward Ellada?"

"That is why I'm out here. Sinth Tyrannus has sent me to tell you to rally up the rainshockers for takeoff."

"So, we're going to Ellada?"

"That we are doing, Jakah." Labara spoke. "Rally them up and prepare them for the travel ahead."

"I will do so."

All of the Viper Order prepared themselves for the travel toward Ellada. Tyrannus and Labara grabbed their gear and their aduroblades. The rainshockers and howlshockers all gathered together into the Attonbitus with Jakah entering his own ship. From the castle doors, come out Tyrannus and Labara. Prepared and ready for the battle. They enter the Sinth-Tred and as soon as its doors shut, the engines begin to roar. Jakah's ship is already hovering in the air, awaiting the Sinth-Tred and Attonbitus to do the same.

The Sinth-Tred lifted into the air and took off, with Jakah and the Attonbitus following. Within mere seconds, they are out of Moraltis and its atmosphere. The ships are now flying through the stellar space, mapping out the precise location on Ellada to make their landfall. Jakah communicates with Tyrannus and Labara through his helmet. They can hear him talking through the holographic monitors on the ship.

"Which way will we make landfall?" Jakah asked.

"We will land right in the heart of their city of Olympya. There, we will spread out and take the battle to them."

"Understood."

The ships flew past the planets of Sinstor and Ivil, making their exit out of the Star 895 sector and outward into the deep stellar space. Tyrannus looked out and he could mostly see all the planets. Each in sectors. Labara looked out as well, gazing at the amount of worlds that are out in the universe.

"Soon, Labara, we will have in our possession each and every one of these worlds."

"On that day, we will certainly be rulers over the universe."

"That, my wife, is the ultimate goal of the Viper Order."

The ships flew through the deep stellarspace. Passing by other sectors in the universe as they reach for Sector 333, where Ellada is located. Once they arrive toward the sector, the ships slowly make their entrance. Seeing the other planets around them such as Erets-Alpha, Helio, Endro, Endor, Tekh, and Shenxia.

"I see the home of out adversaries, beloved." Labara said, pointing out toward the planet of Helio, the home of the Ancient Knights of the Covenant.

"In time, we will overcome them." Tyrannus said in a calm voice. "In time."

Their ships approached Ellada. Tyrannus and Labara are prepared, just as Jakah and the large amount of rainshockers in the Attonbitus. The ships enter the Elladian atmosphere and they enter the skies over the Elladian cities. Tyrannus looked out, seeing the city of Olympya.

"There!" He yelled. "Land this ship right in the heart of their city!"

The Sinth-Tred Aeronaut proceeded to make the landfall in Olympya. Jakah's ship and the Attonbitus followed their landing movements. Meanwhile, on the grounds of Olympya, residents to the city gaze up into the air, seeing the three ships approaching. Most of them yell and scream in fear.

"The Viper Order has come!!!" Yelled out a woman holding her daughter by the arm.

From the Temple of Oros, walked out Herena, Queen of the Herenian Empire and beside her is her daughter, Savan-Nah, Princess of the Herenian Empire. They look up toward the ship and stand still, awaiting for them to make their landing. Both women are dressed in the battle gear, covered in leathery clothing covered with armor. Their swords are on their sides. No fear is shown on their faces. Only the signs of war.

The ships slowly land with the wind blowing around the city and in the faces of Herena and Savan-Nah. The Attonbitis opened and out runs the army of rainshockers. All in a single-filed line, with the plasma-ranges in hand. Behind them run out the howlsoldiers, with the stealth gear and riot weaponry. Jakah exits his ship, with his plasma-range aimed for Herena. Jakah laughed, seeing Herena standing in front of the temple. The Sinth-Tred opened and out walks Tyrannus and Labara. They approach Herena and Savan-Nah with Jakah and the rainshockers following them.

"I see the Viper Order has no respects for the residents of others." Herena said.

"We are not here to discuss architecture, woman." Tyrannus said. "We are here to conquer your planet."

"Really? You seek to overthrow me and my empire? So you can take over Ellada?"

"Why else would we be here this day."

Herena turned to Savan-Nah and nodded. Savan-Nah smiled as she pulled up and raised her sword in the air.

"Marvels!" She screamed.

From behind them and around the temple arrive an army of armored-clad women. They are the Marvels of the Universe. The primary army of the Herenian Empire and led by Savan-Nah herself. Tyrannus looked around the landscape, seeing the Marvels around them. Tyrannus turned to Labara and nodded. Labara turned toward the rainshockers.

"Arms up!"

The rainshockers raised up their ranges toward the Marvels. Jakah kept his range steady on Herena. Tyrannus and Herena locked eyes with each other. Knowing the power that both of them possess. Tyrannus pulled out his aduroblade and Sinthblade.

"Let's begin our war, Queen Herena."

"I thought you would ask hesitantly." She said, raising up her sword.

Labara raised up her aduroblade against Savan-Nah's sword. The landscape was ready for the battle to begin at any moment. Tyrannus, steadily, turned his attention over to Jakah.

"Do it now."

"With pleasure."

Jakah pressed a series of buttons on his wrist, which caused his ship to hover in the air and begin firing at the Marvels, Savan-Nah, and Herena. Causing Tyrannus to send the rainshockers at them. Savan-Nah noticed the rainshockers and waved her arm.

"Marvels! Attack!"

The Marvels let out a yell as they ran for the rainshockers and the rainshockers toward them. Herena and Tyrannus clashed blades with one another as did Savan-Nah and Labara. Jakah hovered up into the air with his jetpack, firing at the Marvels on the ground with his plasma-range. The howlsoldiers move with silence and stealth, making their way through the battlefield, taking down as many Marvels as they possibly could. Jakah continued firing at them from the air.

"They'll never know what hit them." He said.

A twirling sound is heard coming from behind Jakah. As he turned to see what it could be, he noticed it is a gold aduroblade, the blade swiped Jakah's jetpack, causing him to crash onto the ground. Tyrannus noticed and swiped his aduroblade against Herena with much more strength. He went in close and looked into her eyes.

"Where did you get the aduroblade from, woman?!"

"I didn't get one. It belongs to him."

"Him?!"

Tyrannus shoved Herena back against the temple's post and looked behind him, seeing the aduroblade in the hands of a man, dressed in armor with a brown and white tunic and cloak. Dressed as a Knight of the Covenant. Tyrannus stood and faced him.

"You are him." Tyrannus said boldly. "You are Jad Serkelrod. Five generations from Yabel Serkelrod. Son of Mehar Serkelrod."

"That I am." Jad said. "I'm wondering why you're here on Ellada, Viper Lord."

"The same could be asked of you, One of the Avior."

"Tell me, why are you here?"

"That is not the concern as this moment. Since you're here, I can finish what my master tried to do and that is defeat you."

"Sinth Zane didn't have the strength to take me down. What makes you believe you could?"

"Because I am not like my master and the Dekar is stronger with me than it was with my master."

Jad raised up his aduroblade, so did Tyrannus. Both were ready for their fight. One of the Dekar against One of the Avior.

"Let us see if your words speak truth or if they speak deception."

Tyrannus raised up his adorable and approached Jad and the two clashed with their aduroblades, giving off the sound of a booming thunder.

IV
BATTLE OF OLYMPYA

Tyrannus and Jad continued clashing their aduroblades against one another. As they fight, the Marvels of the Universe battle it out against the rainshockers and howlsoldiers. Savan-Nah dueled with Labara as Herena approached the downed Jakah. He looked and saw her standing near him. He chose to let out a small laugh.

"This is unexpected." Jakah said.

"I noticed your weapon was aimed at me. I wasn't pleased." Herena said. "So, why don't you stand up and face me direct rather than behind your boss' back."

Jakah stood up and faced Herena. He tossed his plasmarange to the ground and smacked his fists in his hands.

"I'll face you. Hand to hand."

"So be it, mercenary scum."

Herena lunged toward Jakah with her fist, Jakah caught her fist and jumped over her, kicking her in the head. Herena's head bounced forward and Jakah landed on the ground and tackled her down. He held her down while he pummeled her in the face. Herena took the attacks and tossed Jakah off her with her strength. Jakah scoffed.

"You're stronger than I thought."

"Don't stop and talk now."

They continue their fight as Jad and Tyrannus's fight could be heard throughout the battlefield. Loud booms emitting from countless impacts of the blades. In the midst of the battle, a man came from the mountains with blades of his own. The Marvels knew who he was and cheered at his appearance. The Viper Lords and Jakah were unaware as to who this mysterious stranger was. Jakah kicked Herena to the ground and approached the stranger. He wore a tunic from the waist down, strapped leather boots with metallic plating alongside two armguards similar to the boots. His eyes were yellow like Ellada's sun. He had little to no hair on his head and no beard.

"Who are you?"

"A warrior of the Dodekatheon. You're trespassing on their territory. And mine!"

The warrior lunged at Jakah, attacking and striking with his blades. Jakah flew into the air, knocking the warrior from him. The warrior landed on the ground and threw his blade, impacting with Jakah's jetpack, causing the hunter to crash. The Marvels saw this and praised.

"Cratos!" They yelled. "Cratos!"

Tyrannus kicked Jad in his left knee and elbowed him, staggering the Knight. Tyrannus held his blade higher and forward, rushing toward Jad. Jad flipped over Tyrannus, slashing the Viper Lord's cloak in half. Tyrannus ceased himself in his steps, reaching behind his back, feeling the heat from the burnt cloak. He turned around to see several pieces of it laying on the ground and in front of him by a few feet, Jad stood, twirling his aduroblade.

"You've proven yourself well." Tyrannus said. "A shame such good things must come to an end."

"That's where you're wrong. Things have only just begun."

While the two opposing forces stared one another down, the Marvels were defeating the shockers and Jakah was taken down by Cratos' might. His warrior skills proved too much for a venator such as Jakah. He was not dead, but down. The Marvels cheered their victory due to the assistance of Cratos and Jad. Although, Tyrannus was not done with the Knight just yet. He took the Sinthblade from its sheath and slashed Jad's chest, creating a deep wound. Jad fell to the ground, holding his chest in pain. He did not let out a single sound of agony as Tyrannus stood over him, smiling. Labara ran toward him, pleading they must reach Mount Oros.

"Take that mark as a sign of this battle. For the next time we meet, one of us will die."

The Viper Lords ran from the scene as the Marvels celebrated their victory. Olympya was protected by its own. Jad was helped up by Savan-Nah. Jakah silently returned to his ship, leaving the planet with a few rainshockers with him. While the Elladians took in their victory, Tyrannus and Labara were on their way to seek an audience with the Dodekatheon.

V

THE DODEKATHEON

Sinth Tyrannus and Sinth Labara walked far from the battlefield and reached Mount Oros, the sacred place of all Ellada. Tyrannus gazed up toward the top, which he could not see as it was shrouded by clouds. He pointed toward the top as Labara looked on.

"They're at the top." Tyrannus said. "That is where we must go."

"How will we get there?" Labara questioned, seeing as the mountain is very, very, very tall. "Do we take a ship?"

"We could. But, I prefer we go on foot. With the Dekar guiding us, I'm sure we'll get there faster than most."

Tyrannus and Labara made their move toward the top. Taking each step on foot. Duing their hike, they never grew tired or hungry. Sweat never poured from their skin and their breath was steady. The Dekar preserved them all the way to the top. Once upon the top, they found themselves standing in the center of what appeared to be a judgment room. The room was large and nearly forty stories in height. The walls decorated in gold and burnt brass, layered with lilies and vines. In the midst sat two cauldrons of fire.

"Mighty Gods of Oros!" Tyrannus yelled. "We have come to have an audience!"

The room began to shift and in front of the cauldron opposite of the Viper Lords appeared twelve thrones. Upon those thrones sat the gods of Ellada. The gods of Oros themselves, known as the Dodekatheon. Tyrannus and Labara bowed before their presence, showing honor toward them in reverence of their power and authority over Ellada.

Sitting to the Viper Lords' left were as follows: *Hermaion*, Messenger of the Gods, Elladian God of Commerce, Thieves, Eloquence, and Streets. *Haphaistios*, Elladian God of Fire, Master Blacksmith and Craftsmen of the Gods. *Aphorodita*, Elladian Goddess of Love, Beauty, and Desire. *Areios*, Elladian God of War, Violence, and Bloodshed. *Artemas*, Elladian Goddess of Hunting, Virginity, Archery, Moon, and Animals.

Sitting to the Viper Lords' right were as follows: *Apellaios*, Elladian God of Light, Prophecy, Inspiration, Poetry, Music, and Art. *Athenai*, Elladian Goddess of Wisdom, War, Science, and Literature. *Damater*, Elladian Goddess of Fertility, Agriculture, Nature, and Seasons. *Posieidawon*, Elladian God of the Seas, Earthquakes, and Tidal Waves. *Hestva*, Elladian Goddess of Hearth, Domestication, and Family and *Hora-Uno*, Queen of the Elladian Gods and Goddess of Marriage and Family.

Lastly, sitting in the middle of the pantheon was *Emperor Dyeus*, the Elladian God of Thunder and the Sky, Ruler of Mount Oros. Tyrannus stood up and looked toward the gods of Oros. Their thrones and height were far beyond the Viper Lord's own. He looked at them further.

"I thought there were more of you."

"Two are elsewhere." Dyeus said with a commanding voice. "What brings the servants of The Fallen One to our mountain?"

"We come seeking an alliance."

"An alliance with non-worshipers?"

"This is for a greater cause." Tyrannus added. "We share a common enemy. The Knights of the Covenant. The servants of

The High One."

"The Knights of The High One have never sought to take us out or to destroy our position. We do what we must. What we were placed to do."

"But, these are different times than before. More so than the Cavalier Civil War. These Knights aren't as forgiving and honorable as their ancestors. They're vicious. Whomever they seek to destroy, they do at a quickening pace. You will not see them coming."

Dyeus took in their words, sitting back in his throne as the other gods glared toward the Viper Lords. They could sense the Dekar upon them, searing out with great power. Dark power. Dyeus leaned in forward to the Viper Lords.

"If we aid you, what shall we be given in return?"

"As our Fallen One proclaims, you will receive a great portion of the universe and the sectors you can rule. You can gain more worshippers from across the stars and doing so, will put you and your pantheon atop the universe near our Fallen One."

"He speaks of more worshippers out there?" Hara-Uno asked.

"More servants to our cause will greatly make things better." Dyeus said. "Our work will be seen by all within the sectors. Showcasing our dominance across the stellarspace itself."

"What do you say, Emperor of Oros?" Tyrannus asked. "Will you come to terms from our Fallen One?"

"Your god is clever. But, manages a great strategy of dominance. We shall give it time and speak to your god face to face."

"Understood." Tyrannus said, bowing.

"As we should." Labara added.

"Now, leave us." Dyeus commanded. "Your god will deliver the response to you when it's time."

The Viper Lords left Mount Oros and Ellada, returning to

Moraltis with what was left of their army. Sometime later, during a meditation process with Tyrannus and Labara, they were granted an utterance in the Dekar, signaling the agreement between the Dodekatheon and the Fallen One was in place. Settled in stone across the walls of the Moraltian Castle as well upon the base of Mount Oros.

"It is settled." Tyrannus said.

"Yes." Labara replied. "Our higher learning has begun."

VI

THE COMING HEIRS
349 YEARS DURING THE BATTLE OF CAELUM

Fifty-one years after the Battle of Olympya, the Viper Lords trained and mediated deeper into the Dekar. Many things changed across the sectors as the alliance between the Viper Lords and the Dodekatheon was now known across many nations. The Magus Court later came to terms of an agreement between Ordow and Moraltis.

Labara was in labor and she gave birth to her and Tyrannus' first child. A son. The child was named Cain and proclaimed to become a future Viper Lord. Upon his birth, the Dekar was infused within the infant as his eyes were the colors of a red sky, streaking with lightning. The priests entered the chambers after the birth and praised the child. After the priests gave out their praise, the Supreme Cardinal entered the chamber and gazed upon the son. He bowed and nodded his head.

"The lineage of the Dekar will continue with this one. For I sense the power already surging in him. Lords Tyrannus and Labara, guide him well. Teach him ours ways as you were taught in your youths. Make him love the Fallen One with all his heart. Always let the Dekar guide his footsteps as it has and is guiding yours."

The Cardinal began speaking in Moraltian tongues over

him. Cain was destined to become a powerful Viper Lord.

    Elsewhere, on the planet of Erets-Alpha in the country lands near the city of Coolts, there was a woman giving birth at approximately the same exact time as Labara. This woman was Desta Serkelrod, the wife of Laban Serkelrod, son of Jad. Their child was a son as well and he was called Aweran Serkelrod. Desta smiled as she placed her eyes upon him, proclaiming he is the "beginning restoration". Aweran was destined to become one of the Knights of the Covenant as were his fathers who came before.

VII

THE CONJUNCTION
335 YEARS DURING THE BATTLE OF CAELUM

Tyrannus and Labara traveled to Sinstor to meet with Pharao Khopra-Ahr, the ruler of the Late Period Dynasty of Sinstor. The Late Period came into place after the death of Amran-Em-Of and fall of his New Kingdom. The Viper Lords arrived in Misriaym and entered the palace. They stood before the Pharao in the throne room and showed obeisance toward him. All in honor.

"It is good to see great allies once more." Khopra said.

"We've come to you after we heard word of assistance." Tyrannus said.

"Very well. Then, you know about the Emerald Cavaliers and their interference in Sinstor's growth."

"We've heard the Knights are also involved." Labara said. "What have they done so far?"

"They're aiding the Cavaliers against us. Things aren't as they were during the War of Helio. However, this is a new age and things cannot be ruled the same. So, I ask of you to assist me in countering the attacks of this Cavaliers and the Knights, whom you know much of."

Tyrannus nodded.

"We will aid you, Pharao. For in fact, we are already allies as were the fathers before our time."

"Those who knew what they could achieve." Khopra added. "Yes, we already are."

The Viper Lords left the Pharao's presence and with this alliance, the Pharao commanded his scribes to write down the names of Tyrannus and Labara upon the walls of the throne room, engraving them within the other hieroglyphics across the walls.

VIII

AVIOR VS. DEKAR
325 YEARS DURING THE BATTLE OF CAELUM

Ten years later, Tyrannus and Labara sat in the throne room of the Moraltian Castle, mediating into the Dekar. Over those ten years, the Viper Order increased in strength and power. In the middle of their mediation, they were contacted by their Emperor. He appeared in a dark shrouded mist in their sight. They saw him and bowed.

"We weren't aware of your visitation, master." Tyrannus said. "What is your command?"

"He two of you have grown profoundly in the Dekar. The Viper Order is recognized as a tremendous superpower across the sectors. However, there is another power which rivals ours. The Avior. It is growing as well. Creating a rift through the cosmos. You know what must be done. Go to Helio and eliminate the Knights of the Covenant. Bury the Avior's power for all eternity!"

"We will do as you have spoken." Tyrannus said.

"It will be done, master." Labara added. "We shall not fail."

"I know you won't. Now go."

The mist evaporated as the Lords stood tall. They equipped themselves and the rainshockers. Without haste, they traveled to Helio. Making their landing in the wilderness outside of the city of Tropolton. They knew how to manipulate the radars of the planet to avoid capture. The rainshockers ran out with ranges in hands the Lords exit the ship last. They made their way toward the city and before they could reach it, an aduroblade appeared from the trees, slashing several rainshockers in half. The blade twirled and returned to its user who walked out from the bushes.

"I see." Tyrannus said.

Standing before them was a Knight of the Covenant. Dressed in the same garb as those before. The energy of the blade glowed a dark blue. He stood firm before Tyrannus and Labara.

"You're trespassing."

"And who might you be?" Labara asked.

"I am Laban, son of Jad Serkelrod."

Tyrannus stepped further, pulling out his aduroblade.

"A Serkelrod?! Where is your father?"

"On Knight duty. What's your purpose here, Moraltian?"

"Tell me this, before I kill you, how old are you?"

"How old are you?"

"I'm older than your father. Now you."

"Fifty-five years during this Battle of Caelum."

"Ah." Tyrannus nodded. "Good prime age for a warrior. Howbeit that this day is your last."

"Just get ready to fight." Laban raised his blade.

"Fair enough."

Tyrannus and Laban clashed their blades against each other. The two battled it our within the wilderness as Labara took the remaining rainshockers and headed toward the city. Laban fought with striking blows as Tyrannus moved quickly, swiping his aduroblade toward Laban's knees. Laban raised his hands, using the Avior to blow back the Viper Lord. Tyrannus was impressed at his skills.

"You know how to use your true power."

"When it's necessary."

"What is more necessary than preserving your life!"

Tyrannus forcefully caused a tree to come crashing down as Laban jumped out of its way and collided once more with

Tyrannus, who laughed during the fight. Laban shoved Tyrannus and swiped the blade against the Viper Lord's chest, cutting the armor. Tyrannus nodded with a smirk.

"Oh good." Tyrannus scoffed.

He grabbed Laban and head-butted the Knight. Laban stood up from the blow and they continued clashing the blades. Through the clashes, the blades sparked against one another as the air was being absorbed by them. Laban was losing his breath.

"Can't you count on your Avior to aid you?!"

"Do not mock the power of The High One."

"I'll mock until I'm dead."

"Then, prepare to fall as did your Fallen One!"

Laban pushed back, regaining his breath as he took steps to avoid Tyrannus' incoming attacks. Laban turned, kicking Tyrannus to the ground. He moved and stood over the Viper Lord with his blade over his throat.

"You've lost here."

"Haven't they taught you anything?"

Labara appeared from behind Laban, swiping him in his back with her own aduroblade as Tyrannus shoved him back and rushed him with the Sinthblade, impaling him in the chest. Laban fell to the ground as the Viper Lords stood over him.

"I truly hope your Knights aren't as ceasing as you."

"My bretheren will avenge me as will my son."

"Your son?" Tyrannus asked. "Well, I hope to meet your son. For if I do, he'll soon be joining you in the higher realm."

Laban was dead as the Viper Lords made their way toward Tropolton.

IX
THE GREAT PURGE

    The rainshockers invaded the city of Tropolton as the Knights of the Covenant were caught off guard due to their ongoing conflicts with the Magus Court and concerns surrounding the power of the Dekar across the sectors. Rainshockers shot down and killed anyone who came into their sights. From the Temple of the Avior rushed out the Knights. Those Knights were Nidd Sycl-Derdr, Giphbel Tykm, and Mossh El-Jiad, All armed with aduroblades as they quickly rid of the rainshockers, leaving Tyrannus and Labara last. The three Knights made their moves against the Viper Lords, but they were too inexperienced against Those of the Dekar. They did however fight with great strength and honor, but their focus was scattered in between, saving the people, fighting the Viper Lords, and evacuating the city itself.
    Afterwards, walked out four more Knights. They were led by Amzi Grake. He saw Tyrannus and Labara and went to fight against them. Amzi and Tyrannus fought each other as more rainshockers arrived, giving room for the other Knights to take them out. Labara stood back as she did not want to fight three Knights on her own, as they would've surely taken her out quickly. Amzi was strong naturally and spiritually as the Avior was overtaking the Dekar in the battle and Tyrannus grew tired. Amzi knocked both the aduroblade and Sinthblade from Tyrannus' grasp and decapitated the Viper Lord. Labara

witnessed his head fall from his body and she let out a purging scream of agony. To the point where she took out her own aduroblade and impaled herself. She fell to the ground as the Knights watched her crawl toward her husband as she died by his side.

The city was in flames and more rainshockers were arriving as was more Moraltian enforcements.

"What shall we do?" A Knight said to Amzi.

"We must leave. Return another day."

Amzi led the remaining Knights of the Covenant as they fled into the wilderness of Helio.

X

THE LAST ONES

Upon the treachery and defeat of the Abhdi against the Viper Order, the remaining Knights of the Ancient Covenant fled into the wilderness and hid from the Viper Order and their massive army of Rainshockers. There were four Knights that escaped from the hands of the Viper Order and their leader, Sinth Tyrannus and his wife, Sinth Labara. Tyrannus and Labara fell in battle to the Abhdi Knights. But, it wasn't enough to save the Abhdi Knights themselves. Now, the Viper Order has placed two new Viper Lords in the places of Tyrannus and Labara. Sinth Cain and his wife, Sinth Kara. Their first task is to hunt down the remaining Knights and exterminate them from existence along with their beliefs and sovereign ideals. The four Knights that escaped were Orvan Shackleford, Novad Tengu, Ebed El-Ezer, and their leading Abhdi Master, Amzi Grake.

Walking through the wilderness of their home planet called Helio, a planet that was the homeland of the Old Covenant, a land ruled by sovereignty and peace before it was sacked and taken over by the Viper Lords eons after eons, Amzi leads the remaining Knights through the wilderness, moving quietly as they can to avoid any possible disturbance that could give away their signal to the roaming rainshockers lurking around the forest. Their robes show the signs of war, ripped in parts and burned in others. Blood stained across their loose-fitting pants and chest.

"Master, what is our plan exactly?" Orvan said. "We're nearly exhausted and we don't know if we can move much longer like this."

"Knight Orvan, keep your worrisome words to yourself." Amzi said. "Do not speak of them in such a manner. For what you shall speak will become your reality."

"What of the refugee base out here?" Novad said. "Perhaps we should proceed there to find any aid in our mission."

"You are correct, Knight Novad. Come, let us seek out the refugee base. That way we can regain the strength we've lost in this treacherous battle."

They move on through the wilderness. Ebed pulled Amzi to the side and looked around at the trees.

"Master, the Viper Order will not stop until they've killed all of us."

"I understand that. But, we cannot back down from a fight against them if they happen to come across our pathway."

"They killed three of our brothers in arms."

"I know. I was there when they crossed over. I witnessed it all." Amzi said. "Ebed, you must listen to me, we were promised to live through such circumstances like this one. In time, we will overcome them like our ancient ancestors have done."

Amzi pats Ebed on his right shoulder and smiled. Ebed nodded to Amzi.

"Come on, let's get to that base."

Walking for a few miles through the wilderness, the Knights find themselves looking out toward a small base surrounded by evacuees from Tropolton, the capital city of Helio. They walked toward the base as the people turned and looked upon them. Spotting their robes and their presence, they know they're Abhdi Knights and immediately the people run toward them, begging to know of their cities' current circumstance.

"People of Tropolton, please calm yourself and we will explain all that we know of your city."

"What of our city?'" A refugee said. "What about our families out there?!"

"What we do know is the city has been sacked by the Viper Order." Amzi said. "But, some of our fellow Knights managed to slay Sinth Tyrannus and his wife took her own life afterwards out of fear of imprisonment."

"When can we go back?" Another refugee said. "When can we return to our homes?"

"We do not know if you'll ever return to your homes."

The people gasped in fear and dread of never seeing their homes again. Amzi stood before them and raised his hand. Calming and relaxing them from their fears.

"We will restore Tropolton in time and you'll have your city back and your planet well protected."

"How can you be so sure of that, Knight of Abhdi?" One refugee said. "How can we trust your words?"

"Trust not my words, but the actions that will ensure its protection."

The people stood quiet as Amzi and the Knights continued to walk toward the main section of the base. They sat underneath a tent until nightfall. While sitting, they ate and drank while discussing their next phase of action.

"We'll need some assistance." Amzi said.

"We surely do, Master." Ebed said. "But, I'm not so sure we'll find them here."

"We need younger assistance. Younger warriors that will one day take our place as Knights of Abhdi and bring them into becoming Those of the Avior."

"Are you sure its appropriate that we do such a task now?" Orvad said. "When could we find them?"

"Not sure at the moment." Amzi said. "But, it will come

up when the time is appointed."

After several hours when the people took themselves to sleep and the Knights took some time to rest up, a group of rainshockers slowly made their way into the base wearing their dark gray and white clad armor, they slowly raised up their plasma-ranges and aimed them toward the people sleeping. The commanding rainshocker raised up his hand and moved it down.

"Take the shots!" The Rainshocker Commander said."

The rainshockers started firing at the people who woken up in an instantly screaming in fear. The Knights were also awake and took notice at the rainshockers. They stood up and counted them.

"There's ten of them, Master." Novad said. "What shall we do about them?"

"Eliminate as many as you possibly can." Amzi said. "We're here to protect the people."

The Knights walked out of their tent and pulled out their main choice of weapon from their sides, out of their sheaths, the aduroblade. A weapon similar to a sword, made of minerals from the stars and coated with a plasma energy. Amzi's aduroblade glows blue, Ebed's glows green, Novad's glows yellow, and Orvan's glows orange. They run out into the open and combat the rainshockers, using their aduroblades to block the shots from the rainshockers' plasma-ranges. They ram toward the shockers, swiping off their limbs with the aduroblades and killing them with blows to the abdomen and back. Amzi turned and looked out into the forest, seeing more rainshockers coming their way. He faces the Knights, waving at them to exit the base.

"We have to leave!" Amzi said. "More are coming."

"Master." Ebed said.

The Knights fled the base as about a dozen more rainshockers stormed through the base, killing whomever remained. In the woods, the Knights ran as fast as they possibly could with as little rest they've received. They took a brief moment to catch their breaths as the sounds of the plasma-ranges were fading away in the distance.

"What are we to do now, Master?" Novad said.

"Brothers, it seems that in order to find our new recruits, we'll have to leave Helio and leave here fast."

"Where are we to go?" Orvan said.

"We'll go to Erets-Alpha. I am certain we'll find our young members there. Plus, the planet has a wall that forbids the Viper Order from entering their atmosphere."

"We'll need a ship, Master." Ebed said.

"I know. We'll have to make a quiet return to Tropolton and reclaim our ship."

"Its too dangerous, Master." Orvan said.

"Its our only option as of this moment." Amzi said. "We will return to Tropolton by nightfall, reclaim our ship and leave this planet for Erets-Alpha."

"We understand your words, Master." Ebed said.

Amzi nodded as he and the Knights made their way back toward Tropolton while moving quietly from the surrounding armies of rainshockers.

XI

PREPARE THYSELF

Returning to Tropolton through the wilderness, avoiding the rainshockers that are swarming through the land, Amzi leads the Knights back to the now desolate city and its decimated temple. The Knights take a look around their surroundings, hearing the sounds of the rainshockers' machines walking through the woods, stomping and crushing downed branches, moving through the bushes.

"They brought the Raubtiers with them." Orvad said.

"They were prepared for the battle that they sought." Amzi said. "We have to keep moving. Make our way toward the temple."

Making their move through the woods, a land-veho passes them by, rode by one of the rainshockers. A land-veho is a hovering vehicle similar to a motorcycle without its wheels.

"They have the vehoes with them too." Novad said. "They were prepared."

"They surely were." Amzi said. "Let's keep moving."

The land-vehoes come flying past them through the woods as they made their way through.

On the planet called Moraltis, the home world of the Viper Order, Sinth Cain and Sinth Kara, dressed in their hooded black, scarlet, and red cloaks and armored plated uniforms, sit on their thrones within the Moraltan Castle surrounded by rainshockers and cloaked advisers. Within the throne room, two rainshockers opened the doors, allowing a woman to enter. The woman walked in wearing hunting gear and equipped with a weapon of her own to her side, resembling a bullwhip. She approached Sinth Cain and Sinth Kara.

"Dos Ar-Suyaza." Sinth Kara said.

"Masters." She said.

She kneeled before them at their presence. Showing respect and honor towards her new Viper Lords. Sinth Cain nodded and lifted his hand up toward her. She raised up her head and faced him.

"Rise up, huntress." Sinth Cain said.

"I heard you called to require my assistance in a certain matter."

"We need your assistance on an urgent matter."

"Whatever my masters commands of."

"Good." Sinth Kara said. "Because it requires you to hunt down the remaining Knights of the Old Covenant."

"The Knights? I thought they were all but dead. Sinth Tyrannus and Sinth Labara insured us that he would've killed them all."

"But he didn't, did he?" Sinth Cain said. "Now, the task is in the hands of myself and my wife. We will complete the mission that the previous Lord failed to do."

"Where were they last sighted, masters?"

"On their home world of Helio." Sinth Cain said. "Tropolton is their precious city. They're fully armed with their blades."

Dos nodded in understanding. She looked back at the rainshockers standing by the door.

"If I may ask humbly, masters. I will need a small army of my own to back me up in this bounty of yours."

"Sure." Sinth Kara said. "Take as many shockers as you please. Acquire the resources you will need at completing this task."

"When you make your move onto them. After you've killed them all, bring back their aduroblades as a remnant of their deaths."

"I will do so, masters."

Dos nodded as she left the throne room. Sinth Kara turned to Sinth Cain, smiling at him.

"Soon, my love, we will make a full end of those Ancient Knights and their foolish belief in the *Avior*."

"Do not underestimate the power of the *Avior* or the one who controls it." Sinth Cain said. "It has the power to wipe us all out if its pleased. There's a reason it is known as the adversary to the *Dekar*."

Amzi and the Knights have made it through the woods and into the city of Tropolton. Amzi looks at the city streets, seeing them occupied with rainshockers. Armed with their plasma-ranges and searching every building around them.

"We're gonna have to make a stealth way towards the temple." Amzi said. "Otherwise, we'll end up in a firestorm with them and our blades."

"So, how do we do this, master?" Orvad said.

"Follow my lead and we'll make a straightway towards the temple, gather our gear and get off of this planet."

"As you say." Novad said.

The Knights moved slowly and quietly through the streets. Hiding from the rainshockers on the roads nearby. Moving as fast as they can through the street. They approach the temple steps and open its doors. Making their way inside, they see the damage that was left behind as well as the deceased corpses of their fallen brethren and Sinth Tyrannus and Sinth Labara. Amzi kneeled down at the bodies of his brethren and hung his head before them.

"Farewell, brothers." Amzi said. "We'll see you in the

Next Life."

"What of their bodies, master?" Ebed said. "Shouldn't we bury them?"

"Yeah. We should."

The Knights had taken the time to bury the fallen in a small garden nearby the temple. Amzi grabbed the aduroblades of the fallen brethren and placed them in a vault within the walls of the temple, surrounded by other aduroblades and weapons from previous Knights of the Old Covenant. The Knights gathered the equipment they needed and proceed towards the ship called Helio Sor. A circular ship with a fin atop and two side that looked like wings.

"Ready to leave this place?" Amzi said.

"Ready we are."

They entered the ship and Amzi takes lead. Turning on the ship, its engine roars and gets the attention of the rainshockers, who make their way towards the temple entrance. Orvad looked out of the ship's window, seeing them coming.

"Rainshockers are coming, master."

"Give them a quick fight while the ship prepares herself for liftoff."

Orvad, Novad, and Ebed run down from the ship and begin fighting the rainshockers with their aduroblades as Amzi prepares the ship. Swiping the rainshockers with the blades. The ship roars, signaling its ready for takeoff.

"Come on!" Ebed said. "We have to leave now!"

The Knights run toward the ship, deflecting the firing shots from the rainshockers' plasma-ranges. They jump into the ship as it lifts itself up and bursts through the temple walls and flies into the air, vanishing into thin air with hyper speed. The rainshockers look above, no longer seeing the ship.

"Make sure our outer fleets have their eyes on sight for them." The leading rainshocker said to his group. "We cannot have them running loose out there."

XII

A YOUNG ABHDI

The Knights arrive on the planet of Erets-Alpha. Flying through the air above its primary city of Coolts. The residents look up towards the ship and point. Astonished to see a ship of such valor and detail. The ship flew past the city, near the rural grounds in the outskirts of Coolts.

"Best we make a landing out here rather than near the city." Amzi said. "The crowd could bring us some trouble."

Amzi landed the ship in the middle of the country-like fields away from the city of Coolts. Once they exited the ship, Amzi locked it down and camouflaged the ship into the appearance of being invisible from prying eyes across the country fields. While they walked away and headed toward the nearest home for refugee, Amzi noticed a young man wandering in the woods nearby. The young man dressed in boots, loose-fitting pants, and a medieval style light tan tunic. His short cut black hair stood out from his uniform.

"Do you sense that power, Knights?" Amzi said.

"I sense it." Orvad said. "Where's it coming from?"

Amzi pointed toward the young man in the woods, cutting down bushes with a sword. Amzi stared at him and noticed his techniques with the sword. He could sense the young man had the potential to become one of the Knights of the Covenant or one of the Viper Lords.

"What's your plan with him, Master?" Novad said.

"Remember when I once said we'll need some assistance

on our mission in defeating the Viper Order?"

"We do remember your words."

"That young man is the first step in accomplishing that task."

Amzi walked past the knights toward the woods to greet the young man. The Knights followed him as they came closer toward the woods and the young man. The young man chopped down a small tree and as it fell, he could see Amzi and the Knights approaching him. He stared at them with curiosity, he recognized their uniforms, their cloaks, and their aduroblades on their sides.

"It's them." The young man said.

Amzi and the Knights approach him as the tree fell and they could see the interest in the young man's eyes as he stared at them. Novad looks at the other Knights and turned toward Amzi.

"I think he knows who we are."

"That makes our meet and greet better than what could've happened if he didn't."

Amzi walked toward the young man and extended his hand. The young man shook his hand with a glinting smile coming from his face.

"Why do you smile, young one?" Amzi said.

"I recognize who you are." Aweran answered.

"Do tell."

"You're The Ancient Knights of Elyon. The Knights of the Old Covenant as some would call you."

"So, you know of us." Amzi said. "You know what our mission is in this life and you know what we strive for."

"I've done my study on your mission and what you desire to achieve."

"Is there a place nearby that we could rest at for a moment?"

"You can come to my home. There's enough room for you all."

"Splendid. Lead the way, young one."

The young man led Amzi and the Knights to his home out in the rural lands. Once they approach the home, the young man opened the door and allowed them to enter, which he entered last and shut the door.

"Do any of you require water or food?"

"Water would be well." Amzi said. "So, young one what is your name?"

"My name's Aweran Serkelrod. Named after my great-great grandfather, Judios Aweran Serkelrod."

"I know of him. He was a Knight as well. An Abhdi Knight who fought during the Rise of the Supremacy."

"So I've heard he did. Shame I never had the chance to meet him."

"Someday you will."

Aweran brought the Knights some cups of water, which they drank without hesitation. Aweran noticed the cuts and stains of blood on the Knights' uniforms and cloaks.

"If you don't mind me asking, it appears you guys went through some kind of battle before coming here."

"Our home planet of Helio was attacked by the Viper Order and they sacked our city of Tropolton with their armies of rainshockers. We Knights did our best effort to fight for our city, but it was not enough and we lost three of our brothers in the process."

"I'm sorry to hear that."

Amzi placed his cup onto the table and set an interest into what Aweran knows through his researching.

"Tell me, young one, what do you know about the Knights of the Covenant and the Viper Order?"

"I know that you've fought each other for thousands of years and continue to battle this day. I also am aware that the both of you have the ability to use the *Avior* and *Dekar* to your advantages in battle."

"You know of the Avior and the Dekar?" Novad said.

"How much have you learned from them?"

"I have learned only what I have read. I take it that you Knights can harness the power of the Avior?"

"We surely can and you can too."

Aweran paused for a moment, slightly took a swallow and shook his head.

"I wouldn't know that to be a possibility." Aweran said. "I'm not a knight like you men."

"Tell me this, Aweran, if you were given the opportunity to leave your home and travel with us, we would train you, make you a Knight of the Covenant. An Abhdi Knight. You could help save souls from the Viper Order and bring peace across the universe. Would you turn down such an offer?"

"I wouldn't know what to say if it were to come up."

Amzi nodded. "Aweran, it has come up and I am giving you that opportunity right this moment. By morning, you can come with us and save souls, become a Knight of the Covenant, bring peace to the universe or you can decline such an offer and remain here at your home. An average living where life and death flow through the lands like the winds of the air flow through the trees.

"I wouldn't know what to truly say."

"You have until the sun rises the morrow." Amzi said. "Take your time to meditate on it, your life requires of it."

Amzi and the Knights went into the others rooms of the home and stayed their to rest the entire day. Before the sunset, Aweran gathered the cut down bushes and small trees and carried them near his home where he would used them for firewood. While gathering the wood, he could hear a snarl coming from within the dark woods. Aweran looked around for his sword, but it was in the house, laying near the door.

"Dammit." Aweran said.

From the woods jumped out above Aweran an Oxow, a four-legged beast of great strength, which its hide shined a light brown from the downed sun and the rising moon. The oxow roared at Aweran as it tackled him down to the ground and stood atop him, trying to impale at his neck with its horns. Aweran held the beast above him with his strength and yelled for help.

From the home ran out Amzi, who eyes caught the beast and he pulled out his aduroblade. Aweran threw the oxow off of him and stood up to the beast. He turned around seeing Amzi.

"Aweran, use this!" Amzi said, tossing his aduroblade to Aweran.

Aweran caught the aduroblade and once it was grasped the blade became coated in the blue aura of energy that gave it its power. The oxow lunged at Aweran, its horns straight out, and with one swipe of the aduroblade, the oxow was killed and its body fell to the ground, cut in half as if it was butter to a heated knife.

"Not bad, young one." Amzi said. "Good things it was not an Daseur."

The other Knights walked out of the home to see Amzi and Aweran standing next to the dead oxow. They walked toward them in the field near the woods where they could see Aweran holding Amzi's aduroblade in his hands.

"Why is he holding your aduroblade, Master?" Orvad said. "He's not supposed to use your blade."

"He had no weapon on him when the beast attacked." Amzi said. "The only option was to hand him my aduroblade and through that he survived the attack and killed the beast."

Amzi looked at Aweran with the aduroblade in his hands. He nodded with a grin on his face.

"He also showed he can wield an aduroblade without any problems what so ever."

Aweran handed the aduroblade back to Amzi, who returned it to his side. Aweran looked at the dead beast and gave a circular look around the lands. From the homes around him to the woods behind him. He turned to Amzi after gazing around the land.

"What is it, young one?" Amzi said.

"You know, I've always wondered what my life should be. The path that is. When I held your aduroblade, I felt a presence. Similar to that of my father and his father before him. I should become a Knight like the forefathers of old."

"Does that mean you have answered the opportunity?"

"It has. I'm coming along with you."

Amzi smiled and hugged Aweran with great energy.

"Splendid! You have much to learn, young one."

Amzi and Aweran returned to the home with the Knights following them. They took the dead body of the oxow and burned it as an offering to The High One, to watch over them and give them more power through the use of the *Avior*. The smoke of the offering arose into the air, touching the dusk sky.

Miles away from Erets-Alpha, Dos Ar-Suyaza and her small army of rainshockers landed on Helio and entered the city of Tropolton. She commanded the rainshockers to search the temple for any sign of the escaped Knights. Meanwhile, she walked around the place and could sense the aura of the former Viper Lords.

"So, this is where you both passed on." Dos said. "A place that wasn't a part of your beliefs nor your ambitions."

She could see the stains of their blood on the golden floors of the temple. She rubbed them with an handkerchief and placed it into her pants pocket. From the temple doors came the rainshockers.

"What have you found?"

"Nothing." A rainshocker said. "No sign of the Knights were found around here."

"Are you sure of that?"

"We are positive. They had to have escaped and left the planet."

Dos nodded and walked past the rainshockers toward the outside. Her anger could been seen on her face and felt in the hearts of the rainshockers.

"Looks like we have more lands to search."

XIII

AREA 6776

The following morning on Erets-Alpha in the rural area, Aweran prepared his gear as he walked with the Knights toward their ship, which was parked in the distance from Aweran's home. As they entered the ship, Aweran approached Amzi.

"So, may I ask where are we headed?"

"We will need more young recruits to aid us in this quest. We're going to pay 6776 a visit."

"Area 6776?" Aweran said. "Isn't that a infamous prison planet for bounty hunters and mercenaries?"

"It is." Orvad said." "A place where many do not return to their natural state."

"We need a man there. His cunning ability can prove to be of great use and would bring confusion upon the Viper Order."

"How will we know who to look for, Master?" Novad said.

"It's simple, we'll walk in and ask for his name."

"You know his name already, Master?" Orvad said.

"I do. I know him as well. We have a history with one another that contains a smuggling act he did back in Tropolton. This will be him paying me back for saving his life the last time we met."

"Is he a nice guy?" Aweran said.

"He's a cynical one. Sarcasm is his second language."

Amzi approached the pilot seat and prepares the ship for takeoff. The Knights and Aweran buckle up in their seats, sitting across from each other in rows as the ship slowly hovers and takes off into the air. Aweran looked through the window, seeing his home, possibly for the last time as he looked toward the sky, seeing the blue with the clouds as it evaporated away into a deep darkness where only the dots of the stars could be seen.

Another ship flew through the stellarspace, within the ship walked Dos Ar-Suyaza as she spoke with Sinth Cain through a red hologram projector. She had told him there were no signs of the Knights back on Helio in Tropolton.

"They will not be far, huntress." Sinth Cain said. "I suggest you keep looking and search the place where they would last be seen by prying eyes."

"I will do so, master."

"Make your Viper Lords proud, huntress. Show the Viper Order that you are worthy of your place with us."

"I will."

Sinth Cain's hologram disappeared as Dos walked toward the piloting rainshockers. She stood behind them, gazing out into the abyss of space. Seeing nothing but the stars and distant planets.

"Make way for 6776." Dos said.

"Why would we need to go there." The pilot said. "What would even make it believable to find the Ancient Knights there?"

"Trust me. We make way for Area 6776."

"Yes ma'am." The second pilot said. "On route to Sector 6776. One way."

The Helio Sor makes its way closer to Area 6776 to where Aweran and the Knights are able to see the prison planet in the distance from the ship. Amzi pilots the ship toward the planet. Orvad sat next to Aweran to ask him questions concerning the task.

"If you could choose between the Avior or the Dekar, which would you prefer?"

"How can I answer a question like that?"

"It's a question you answer from the mind. The heart will automatically submit to the Dekar because its comfortable and easier. The Avior takes much work to gain and to keep. I hope for your sake, young one, you gain the Avior and will be able to stand on the frontlines of war with us."

"Time will only give us that answer, Knight Orvad."

"I am well certain of that."

After about twenty minutes, Amzi speaks to Aweran and the Knights that the ship is about to land on Area 6776. The Knights prepare themselves and place their audroblades to their sides.

Aweran looked around and possessed no weapon of his own. Reaching to his sides.

"Master Amzi, I have no weapon of my own."

"You'll have a weapon of your own eventually." Amzi said. "Trust me."

Amzi flies the ship through the lines of the prison planet and prepares to land in the rugged lands near the entrance to the prison. Upon landing, Aweran and the Knights exited the ship and approach the entrance doors and were stopped by 6776 patrolmen.

"What is your business here, gentlemen?"

"We are here to pick up a prisoner." Amzi said. "He is needed of great importance to a major cause."

"Is that all your business requires here?"

"That is our business here. We'll pick him up and we'll be gone."

The patrolmen moved to the size, giving them entrance into the prison. Amzi nodded as they walked through the entrance doors and into the prison. Within the prison structure, they noticed cells of a vast number, ranging from floors from where they stood to floors deep beneath the planet grounds.

"Do you know which floor he is on, master?" Orvad said.

"I do not know." Amzi said. "I will ask the lady at the counter there. She will tell us."

Amzi approached the counter and the lady startled when she looked up toward him. He could sense that she knew he was an Abhdi Knight of the Covenant. He raised his hand up. Open. Commanding her to stay silent in order to avoid patrolmen near the counter. She nodded.

"Do not say a word, my lady. We present to you no harm."

"May I ask why you're here?"

"We're here to pick up a prisoner."

"The name please?"

"Evad Nod."

"The smuggler?" The receptionist said bluntly.

"Yes, my lady."

"Will his weapons be picked up in this matter?"

"Most certainty." Amzi said. "Where he's going, he will need them."

The woman looked onto the computer monitor on her desk. She handed Amzi a card, which he took and looked at it, seeing it marked with numbers and codes.

"Evad Nod is placed on the third floor beneath us. You can go down there and pick him up yourselves if you like."

"We will do so. Thank you for your assistance, my lady."

Amzi lead Aweran and the Knights down to the elevator. They entered and Amzi placed the card within the slider and typed in the floor number. The elevator doors closed as they slowly went down to the third floor.

"Do you feel something going on around here, Master?" Aweran said.

"There are many things that take place here, Aweran. Things that would make the heart of a man or woman cold and cruel."

They make their stop on the third floor and the elevator doors opened, revealing the floor covered with patrolmen walking down the corridors. Amzi looked around.

"Which way do we proceed?" Orvad said.

"Follow me and we'll be just fine."

They walked out of the elevator and down the first corridor, where Amzi looked at the card, which contained the number of the corridor and cell block where Evad was kept. While they walked down the hall, they passed by a woman. Her aura connected with Aweran, who stopped and stared at her. She looked at him and directed her eyes toward the cell and to Amzi. Aweran nodded and stopped Amzi.

"Master, she is being kept her on wrong charges."

"What makes you say that, Aweran?"

"Her aura, I can sense it. She's been wrongly placed here."

"Let me ask her."

Amzi stepped back and faced the woman in the cell. She looked at him with hope in her eyes. Amzi could also sense her aura coming through the cell. He nodded with a smile on his face. He turned to the Knights.

"We have another one, Knights."

"How are we to get her out of here, master?" Ebed said.

"We'll have to get Evad out first. We'll come back for her once Evad is out of the cell. Then we'll make our leave."

They continued walking down the corridor until they stopped at the cell where Evad was kept. Amzi stood in front of the cell, seeing Evad, sitting down with his head turned toward the wall. Amzi tapped on the cell bars to get his attention. Evad waved his hand at him.

"Go away, jack off. I do not want to be bothered by you totalitarian idiots."

"We're not totalitarian as you might know, Mr. Nod." Amzi said. "Turn yourself around to the cell bars and see."

Evad turned to the cell door, seeing Amzi he sood up and approached the cell bars with a smile on his face.

"Great to see you, Amzi."

"Like old times you would say."

"In a matter of speaking." Evad said. "Except this time, you're not on the other side of the cell with me."

"I've changed my ways, old friend."

"You sure have. Why have you come to visit me?"

"I'm here to give you your release."

"My release?"

"I need your assistance in an urgent matter taking place across the universe. Your skills are heavily needed."

"Fair enough. Just get me out of here so I can get my shit back."

"I can tell they have your range?"

"They surely do. They keep it locked in with these other stooges' gear. Mashed around, but I'll know it when I see it. My initials are carved on the handle."

Amzi nodded sarcastically, "Interesting."

Amzi placed the card into the cell door's slider and it unlocked the cell, releasing Evad, who moved out of the cell quickly and looked around the corridor.

"Where are the patrolmen?"

"Walking about their business. No need to worry of them."

"Are you sure about that?"

"I am. Right now we need to get someone else out of this place."

"What someone else?"

"A woman wrongly placed here."

"Now that is something of a discussion. Did you know there are more women imprisoned in this place than men."

"I can speculate as to why."

"I'm sure you can. You know a lot about the life we all live in."

"I don't know a lot, Evad. I know enough to continue living in the right place of mind."

They walked down the corridor, returning to the woman's cell. When Amzi stood in front of the cell bars, the woman's face began to glow with joy. Amzi could sense her happiness rising from within her.

"Don't you worry, young lady." Amzi said. "We're getting you out of here too."

"Isn't that card only designed to release Evad from his cell, master?" Orvad said.

"It is programmed that way." Amzi said. "Though, I made some minor changes to it when she handed it to me."

"What kind of changes?" Evad said. "I'm intrigued to know."

"I'll tell you another time. You might end up here again you know."

"Real funny of you, old friend."

Amzi slid the card into the slider and opened the cell doors for the young lady, who ran out and hugged Amzi. Startling Evad and the Knights, though Aweran smiled at her, recognizing her beautiful features.

"Thank you." She said to Amzi. "Thank you."

"You're very welcome, my lady. We'll need to get you out of here as fast as possible."

"I understand."

"I'll go and get my gear." Evad said to Amzi. "I'll meet you guys out in the parking field."

"Do hurry."

"I surely will."

Evad walked through the corridor and found himself surrounded with patrolmen in every corner.

"I'll be damned."

A few patrolmen approached him. Evad smiled as he walked toward the elevator, going back up to the top floor. The patrolmen continued to look on toward him as the elevator doors closed.

"I'm a free man gentlemen." Evad said. "Can't place me back in your cells."

"What's that supposed to mean?" A patrolman said.

"Just some cocky prick." Another patrolman said.

Amzi, Aweran, and the Knights lead the young woman toward the elevator, passing by the patrolmen. They noticed the young lady with them and stepped in fromt of Amzi.

"Why is she out of her cell?"

"We came here to bail her out."

"That's not what the upper office sent to us. You were sent to release an Evad Nod."

"That is true, but, we're getting a double release this day. Evad Nod and this young lady. Check your system to see the information."

The patrolmen gazed at the monitor, searching the information. After reading it, they turned to Amzi and nodded.

"Our apologizes, sir."

"It is all well." Amzi said. "You were just doing your job."

On the upper floor, Evad walked toward the closet section, where the equipment and gear that belongs to the prisoners is being kept. He searched the closet, which was designed in an alphabetical fashion.

"Where are the Ns?" Evad said. "I am looking for the Ns."

He walked through the closet, until finding the N section and looked through the drawer, finding his black hat, black trench coat, and range, an energy blasting pistol.. Evad smiled.

"Finally. My baby back into my hands."

Evad put on his belt and holster, where the range went. He put on his trench coat and hat and exited the closet section. Upon exiting the closet, Evad noticed Dos Ar-Suyaza standing at the counter speaking with the woman at the desk, behind the woman stood four rainshockers.

"This isn't a good sign."

"May I ask who you are looking for?" The woman at the counter said.

"I am wondering if any gentlemen came pass here." Dos said. "They wore robes with cloaks. One in particular speaks in a philosophical manner."

"Yeah. We did have some men walk in that fit the description."

"Where have they gone?"

"They were down on the third floor."

"Thank you very much."

Evad went to the elevator and before the doors closed, Dos and the rainshockers walked in and stood next to him. The elevator doors shut as Evad stared at Dos and the rainshockers.

"Looks to me like someone is in trouble." Evad said.

Dos looked at him with disgust, to which Evad only smiled at her.

"It is none of your concern, enashian." Dos said. "I am on orders from a high source."

"I can tell. You have his shockers walking alongside you to your command."

"What do you know of rainshockers?"

"I know they can be a pain in the ass for one."

Dos smirked. Taking some little enjoyment out of

Evad's sarcasm.

"Tell me, have you seen any Knights roaming around here?"

"Not to my understanding."

"Are you sure you're telling me the truth?"

"Basically I can say that I am."

On the third floor, Amzi and the Knights stood in front of the elevator doors, awaiting for them to open. Aweran stood next to the young lady, interested in speaking with her.

"You can say something." She said.

"Oh. I didn't want to just start talking out of nowhere is all."

"What is your name?"

"Aweran Serkelrod. You can just call me Aweran. What is your name?"

"Zeena Lyh, I'm from the planet Endor."

"The planet where the Carus Sword is kept hidden?"

"Yeah. I've seen the ancient home of the legendary Siegfried-Ard."

"What's it like?"

"It's a calming place. The peace there is nice until its trampled upon by outsiders seeking the Carus Sword."

"Do you know where the sword is located?"

"No. but I've heard its buried beneath the Conscendo Sceleratus."

"The mountain of the Ard Family."

"Yeah."

The elevator doors opened and both side were immediately at arms with each other. Amzi looked at Evad in the elevator, standing on the side of Dos.

"What is going on, Evad?"

"Tell me about it."

Dos stepped out of the elevator and faced the Knights with the rainshockers surrounding them. She smiled as she looked into the eyes of the Knights and stopped on Amzi.

"The legendary Amzi Grake." Dos said. "It is a pleasure to meet you finally."

"Who are you, huntress?"

"You may call me Dos Ar-Suyaza. I am here on duty for the Viper Order. Sinth Cain and Sinth Kara require that I eliminate you and your fellow brethren from existence."

"You will find out that it isn't an easy task to accomplish."

"I'm aware of that, Abhdi Knight."

"KNIGHTS!" Amzi yelled, with the knights raising up their aduroblades.

The Knights slaughtered the rainshockers within seconds with the aduroblade as Aweran and Zeena stood back from the fight. Evad signaled to them to enter the elevator. They ran for it while the Knights fought off the patrolmen. Once the patrolmen were defeated, Aweran and Zeena made it to the elevator. They now awaited Amzi and the Knights to enter. In their way stood Dos, who reached to her side, revealing an adurowhip in her possession. The adurowhip was made of a metallic leather material and glowed a neon blue and was surging with energy. Amzi nodded at her while gazing at the whip.

"You came prepared, huntress."

"As I always do."

Dos swung her adurowhip across the floor around the Knights as they fought off the whip with the aduroblades. They ducked and swiped the Dos' adurowhip several times to avoid an attack.

"Go to the ship!" Amzi said. "We'll be there shortly!"

"Are you sure, master?" Aweran said.

"I am sure. Now go."

The elevator door shut while the Knights battled Dos.

She swung her adurowhip toward Ebed's aduroblade, which wrapped around it. Ebed pulled his blade closer, pulling Dos near them. Novad ran toward Dos and smacked her in the head with his forearm. Dos fell to the ground, releasing the grip on the adurowhip, which fell to the ground.

"Let's go." Amzi said.

The Knights went through the elevator, making their way to the ship. Aweran, Zeena, and Evad stood by the ship, awaiting Amzi and the Knights to approach them.

"What's taking them so long?" Evad said. "They should've been out here by now."

"Give them a few moments." Aweran said. "They'll be here soon."

"I hope so. Wait, who the hell are you, kid?"

"Someone they need for assisting their mission."

"Is that right?"

"It is. Ask them when they get here."

"I will. We'll see which of us they'll need the most."

"That right?"

"Damn right, kid."

"Don't start some competition over who is needed the most while I'm around." Zeena said. "Keep yourselves focused on the real issues."

"Fair enough." Aweran said.

"Yeah." Evad said. "Listen to the lady, kid. You can learn something from a woman."

"As if you would know."

"I know as much as I need to know."

"Ugh, enough." Zeena said. "Quit your bickering."

From the entrance doors came Amzi and the Knights, who ran toward the ship. The ship opened, which Aweran, Zeena, and Evad entered into it with the Knights following.

"Its about time you guys showed up." Evad said. "Can we leave this damn place now?"

"Surely." Amzi said. "Everyone buckle yourselves up.

We're going hyper speed in a matter of moments."

While the ship began to hover into the air above the prison, Dos walked outside and seen the ship above her.

"Damn Knights!" She yelled as the ship flew away into hyper speed.

XIV

THE INWARD BEING

With the Helio Sor flying through the outer depths of space on autopilot, Amzi walked toward the middle of the ship where the Knights sat with Aweran, Zeena, and Evad.

"Aweran and Zeena, come over here." Amzi said. "I have much to discuss with the two of you."

Aweran and Zeena sat in the front of Amzi with the Knights sitting behind him and Evad sitting next to the pilot door, chewing some gum that was left in his belt pocket.

"There is a reason why the two of you were chosen. Evad is a needed ally of course, but you two, I can sense the power of the Avior within you both. You just need to learn of its use."

"What do you mean we have the Avior within us?" Zeena said. "I've never heard much of this Avior."

"Now you have that opportunity, young lady. An opportunity that will change your life into something greater than your mind could possibly comprehend."

"What should we know of the Avior, Master?" Aweran said.

"First things is you both must learn how to communicate with it. The Avior speaks to you in your mind and gives you guidance in all of your ways. With its guidance, you can accomplish great things in your lives and make others better for it."

"That is why I turned it down some years back." Evad

said smacking on his gum. "I can't help but scoff at the idea of helping others when they never helped you in a circumstance."

"You're a smuggler, old friend." Amzi said. "That is why you've never come to learn of the power of the Avior."

Evad laughed hysterically. "No disrespect of course, but I'd rather have my trust in my range rather than pocus spiritualism and ancient weapons."

"In time, you will learn how often the Avior has spared your life from those who possess the Dekar."

"When I do, old friend, let me know."

"What is with your attitude?" Aweran said to Evad.

"There's nothing wrong with my attitude, boy." Evad said. "Maybe you should learn from me one thing in particular."

"What is that?"

"Don't give a shit about anybody but yourself and your deeds. That is the only way you'll stay focus on the matters that truly need managing."

Amzi shook his head and glanced at the Knights, who are already tasting distain at the sight of Evad Nod. Evad looked toward them and nodded his head sarcastically.

"You'll have to deal with me until your little mission is complete, boys."

On the other side of outer space, Dos makes her return to Moraltis, where she stands in the throne room facing Sinth Cain and Sinth Kara. Both of whom look at her with questioning.

"Huntress, have you completed the task which was given into your hands?" Sinth Cain said.

"I found the Knights as you both requested, masters."

"So, where are their remains, huntress?" Sinth Kara said. "What of the whereabouts of the Knights' aduroblades?"

"The Knights were more powerful than I perceived them to be. They showed no fear and took out the rainshockers that came along with me in a quickening. I took it to fight them myself, but they overpowered me and knocked me unconscious."

"The Knights are still free, roaming the universe is what you're telling us, huntress?"

"That I am telling you both, masters."

Sinth Cain stood up slowly from this throne and approached Dos. He walked around her, circling her body, rubbing his hand around her blue hair and slowly touching her bluish pale skin. Sinth Kara turns her head away at the sight of Sinth Cain's doings.

"I am a merciful ruler, huntress." Sinth Cain said. "I will give you another opportunity at completing this task we've given you."

"I will highly appreciate that, masters." Dos said. "But, I will require another army to accompany me."

"Since the rainshockers weren't up to good use for you, take some of the howlshockers. Their stealth and aerial techniques should prove of a highly good use of searching those Abhdi Knights out from their secret place."

Dos bowed her head toward Sinth Cain and Sinth Kara, "Thank you, masters. I will not let you down this time."

"Please don't, huntress." Sinth Kara said. "Because I will not hesitate at striking you down and going after the Knights with my own power. The Dekar flows through me as of my own blood. Its power gives me the thirst for combat and the lust for murder. If you do not return here with their aduroblades as proof of the Knights' deaths, I will end your life quickly and I shall hunt down those Ancient Knights myself and give pleasure to the Dekar."

"I understand."

Dos left the throne room and outside in front of her ship stand an army of howlshockers, dressed in their black and gray uniforms with their militarized goggled helmets, their eyes covered in shadow. Their weapons are solid black and are covered with cloaking tech. After Dos left the throne room, Sinth Cain turned to his wife. She looked at him and could sense the Dekar flowing through him. Rising up within his being.

"The next time you let your tongue roam free in such a manner in front of me, it will be the last thing you decide to do in my presence."

"Do you not understand that I am your wife, Cain. We both are equals in this matter of the Viper Order. We are both Viper Lords and our armies obey us, not one or the other."

"You do not know your place truthfully."

"Don't speak of truth, Cain. As if you are the prime example of such a thing."

Sinth Cain stood up from his throne seat and left the throne room, leaving Sinth Kara by herself as she mediated on the words she and Cain spoke to each other.

Back on the Helio Sor, the Knights speak with Aweran and Zeena about the use of the Avior and the power that it brings upon those who receive it. Novad tells them of the way in acquiring the Avior.

"Die to ourselves?" Aweran said. "How are we to do that?"

"It is an obstacle that lies within you as it does with all living beings in the universe." Novad said. "Once you die to yourself and mortify the deeds of the body, you will receive the Avior and you will have power beyond what you can comprehend."

"How long would such a thing take?" Zeena said.

"It depends on how long you choose to not die to yourselves. Its all in your doing and in your power."

"Sometimes we call the Avior the inward being." Ebed said. "Because it truly lives within you and will truly guide you in all your steps."

"How would we know that we're received the Avior within us?" Aweran said.

"You will begin to speak in a language not known of any living beings within the universe. It is a language from the High Place."

"The High Place?" Zeena said. "What High Place are you speaking of?"

"Caelum." Amzi said. "He's speaking of the high planet that we call Caelum, which is currently at war with a malevolent entity who desires to claim the universe and all life for himself."

"Have any of you been to Caelum?" Aweran said.

"Some of their friends have been there and are still there." Evad said. "I'm sorry, but it is the truth."

"It is best that you keep your mouth closed until you are spoken to, old friend." Amzi said. "Do not utter another word or I will shut your mouth permanently."

"Fair enough, old friend. I need to eat and drink my fill."

Amzi turned from Evad and back to Aweran and Zeena with a smile on his face.

"Aweran and Zeena, in time when we have fully trained you in the arts of the Avior and when you both receive it within yourselves, then we will present to you to true weapon of an Abhdi Knight."

Amzi commanded the Knights to make some space in the room of the ship and handed Aweran his aduroblade and Ebed gave Zeena his aduroblade. They both stood in the middle of the room with Evad watching from a distance. Amzi stood by them, fixing their stance as they held the aduroblades in their hands.

"What you both hold in your hands are the true

weapons of an Abhdi Knight." Amzi said. "The aduroblades are an ancient invention, created during the beginnings of the Battle of Caelum and are still in use to this day. It is known the aduroblades were first created for the Celestials of Caelum. The aduroblades were carry are physical replicas of their own blades."

Aweran and Zeena slowly move around their wrists to gain some balance and control with the aduroblades. Amzi and the Knights watch on while Evad placed his hat over his face, falling asleep.

"You'll need to keep your balance tightly when holding an aduroblade." Amzi said. "For if you were to make a single mistake, it could cost you your life and you could be on your way to Caelum for all eternity. That is if you possessed the power of the Avior within your being of course."

Colliding the two aduroblades against each other. Giving off the sound of a miniature spark with thunder. The flashing light in between the aduroblades gives off the sensation sound of fire meeting energy. They collide the blades again, learning the ways of aduroblade combat.

"Slowly now." Amzi said. "You're not trying to kill each other."

"Yes, Master." Aweran said. "Why do I feel as if I'm losing a little bit of my breath, Master?"

"The more the blades come into contact with each other, the more oxygen they absorb from the close areas surrounding them. If you were to be in a fight for a period of time, you could lose your breath from the blades."

"Seriously?" Evad said.

"A side effect that comes from the energy coating the blade."

Evad shook his head, whistling from what Amzi had said.

"It's a damn good thing I prefer ranges over ancient blades."

Aweran and Zeena continue to make slow collisions with the aduroblades, learning the ways. Ebed approached Amzi as the training continued.

"Where are we headed, Master?"

"We're going to Dagobar." Amzi said. "We need some weapons to be made."

"Do you think the Grogok Clan will bother to listen to us?" Ebed said. "To make weapons for us?"

"I know they're in a civil war with a neighboring clan." Amzi said. "It shouldn't be much of a problem if we were to give them little assistance in their war."

"I understand your words, Master. How far until we reach Dagobar?"

"Within several hours."

Ebed sat back in his seat as he, Amzi, and the Knights continued to watch Aweran and Zeena learn the arts of the aduroblade. Evad sat by himself in the corner of the room, asleep in a chair. Snoring away.

On the other side of space, Dos flies along the stars in her ship with her new army of howlshockers. The howlshockers cover the entire grounds of the ship from the top to the bottom. The lieutenant howlshocker approached her in the pilot room.

"My lady."

"What have you of information, lieutenant?" Dos said. "Have you located the Knights' location?"

"Not any sort of information yet, my lady. But we have detected some strange energy coming from a distance afar off."

Dos turned to the lieutenant. Intrigued at his words declaring energy afar.

"What kind of energy have you possibly discovered out here in the dark abyss?"

"According to our radars, the energy appears ancient. Very ancient and we're on its trail as we speak."

"It may be them after all." Dos said. "We'll keep tracking this energy signature. It may lead us to those Ancient Knights."

The lieutenant howlshocker saluted and walked away from the pilot room near the other howlshockers in waiting. Dos continued to sit in the pilot seat, placing the ship onto autopilot. She smirked at the possible thought of being on the trail of the Knights and their ship.

XV
NEGOTIATIONS WITH THE ORCHS

The Helio Sor made it way toward the planet of Dagobar within Sector V. A planet covered in lush grasslands and jungles, surrounded with various species of animals and mostly dominated by the Orchs and the Trolls. The Knights look out of the windows of the ship, seeing the greenness of the planet shining through its atmosphere.

"Why are we heading there, master?" Novad said.

"We will need their assistance in the art of weaponry." Amzi said. "They are the best blacksmiths within this galaxy are they not, Knight Novad."

"You have a point, master."

"What kind of weapons will they be making, master?" Orvad said. "Are they for us against the Viper Order?"

"The weapons are for our two young apprentices."

Aweran and Zeena looked at Amzi with a glisten in their eyes. Unaware of the idea of being presented weapons at an early stage in their training.

"Are you sure we'd be needing those weapons at this stage in our training?" Aweran said hesitantly. "We haven't even hit the higher basics yet."

"That is what the outside field is for, Aweran. You will know how to use the *Avior* and its powers when you are on the field facing the enemies whom you have not known."

"Are we going to be on the field on Dagobar?" Zeena said. "Along with the Orchs and their civil war?"

"That is a possibility that may surely come to pass, my lady. Don't fear the possibility of it. Embrace it so that you can fully learn what it means to be a Knight of the Covenant."

Flying through the Dagobar atmosphere, coming down to the ground, which is covered with hovels and wooden home along with a castle made of a mixture between brick and wood. As the ship hovers down, the Orchs of the Grogok Clan walk out of their homes, wearing fur tunics and apparel. Their skin is gray, almost pale-like and their fangs appear to sit on the outside of their mouths. Their leader, Grodak'Krak walks outside and gazes up toward the ship. He raises up his steel polished sword, slightly covered with dried blood and mucus.

"Who dares invade our land and enters our planet unaware?!" Grodak yelled.

The ship landed on a cliff in front of the Grogok land. The Knights walked out of the ship, with their hands slightly to their sides near the aduroblades. awe ran and Zeena exited the ship. Evad was still asleep until Amzi walked toward him, shaking him.

"Wake up, old friend. We've landed."

"Oh. Well, where are we?"

"Take a look for yourself. You'll be delighted to know."

Evad stretched over toward the closest window he could get to in his seat. Looking outside he immediately sees the Grogok Castle and jumps out of his seat as if electricity had flowed through his body from a lightning bolt. His hat falling to the ship floor, which he picks up and holds looking back at Amzi with a slight sense of fear and anger.

"Why in the hell are we here?!" Evad said. "Dagobar?! Seriously?!"

"It's an important matter why we're here. Calm yourself, old friend. They will not harm you unless you've done something to them of course."

"I haven't done anything to these orchs. But, I know of their savage civil war. Out of all the planets that are out there, you choose to come here. Abyssus would've been a better place to visit than this."

"I wouldn't be so sure of that, old friend. Dagobar is much more peaceful than Abyssus."

Amzi walked down the steps of the ship with Evad following him, placing his hat onto his head. He walked outside and gazed at the amount of orchs that stood in front of them on the near ground. Evad reached slowly for his range, but Amzi stopped his hand from getting any further.

"Don't you try something stupid, Evad."

"One shot and this can change at the blink of an eye."

"Do not dare to accomplish that idea."

"I'm just being on guard. That's all, old friend."

Amzi moved his hand and continued walking ahead with Evad behind him, his eyes locked on the orchs and their leader. They reached the ground, immediately being surrounded by the orchs. Male, female, children of all shapes and sizes as Grodak'Krak approached the Knights with his sword in hand.

"I recognize such a garb." Grodak said. "You're from the planet called Helio."

"That we are, King Krak." Amzi said. "We are Abhdi Knights of the Covenant. Masters of the Avior. We have come to your planet on an urgent mission and request your assistance in a simple task."

"What task may be of simple reasoning if you couldn't do it yourselves or with your unseen power?"

"Your clan possesses the best blacksmiths of any planet in the universe. We have come to assist an aid in building new weapons for our two young recruits that we have with us."

Grodak leaned his head over Amzi, looking past him toward Aweran and Zeena. He pointed toward them to come forward, to stand next to Amzi, which they did and stood next to him. Grodak measured both Aweran and Zeena with his sword, waving it around their bodies, measuring their height and arm length.

"These two are Knights of your Covenant as well?"

"They are becoming Knights, King Krak. They will need the appropriate weapon in their defense if they were to become Knights of the Covenant."

"You speak of your energy blades."

"That I do."

Grodak nodded and allowed Amzi and the Knights to enter his castle. They followed him to the inside where they seen the filth of an orch. The amount of trophies that were kept from their enemies troll and orch alike. Some were trophies of gigantic birds and large beasts that roam the planet. Evad looked at the trophies and smiled.

"Looks like you have quite the collection, King Krak."

Grodak looked at Evad and turned to Amzi, with concern in his eyes.

"Who is this man that has come along with you?"

"He is Evad Nod. A smuggler of sorts. He will be no harm toward you or your clan. Trust my word on that. Otherwise, if he were to do something, you could take care of him yourself."

"Old friend, that isn't necessary."

"It is of necessity if he wishes to have my aid!"

Evad placed his hands up and kept quiet while Grodak lead them toward the blacksmith area of the castle. Walking down a set of stairs, they approach a door, made of wood, which enters into the blacksmith room. Inside were an variety of swords, war hammers, crossbows, machetes, knives, and other sorts of weapons required of the orch's use.

"There is a problem that we have discovered, Knight."

"What problem would that be?"

"We require the usage of the star matter."

"The star matter?" Aweran said. "What is that, master?"

"The star matter is what the energy weapons are primarily made up of. Such is our aduroblades of course."

"You'll have to find some and bring it back to me. That way, I know I can fully trust you and you will have your weapons in no time."

"I wouldn't know where to look for such a particle."

"But, I know of a place, Knight. A place that I wouldn't even dare to step my feet upon its ground or lick its soil."

"What kind of place is it?" Evad said cautiously. " if I may ask?"

"You will have to enter the planet of Ordow to retrieve such a particle, Knight." Grodak said. "That is the last place that I have knowledge of where a star matter is located. In the possession of the Magus Court and the Warlocks of the West Wind."

"The Magus Court has the matter." Amzi said. "I don't know how we can achieve the matter, but we will give it a go."

"A go you will give to it." Grodak said. "I hope you return in one piece and in safe keepings, Knight."

Grodak nodded and allowed them to leave the castle and return to their ship. Once outside, awe ran began to question Amzi of the planet Ordow, the Magus Court, and the Warlocks of the West Wind. Amzi didn't want to give Aweran the answers immediately, but understood that its best for him to know if they enter combat with the Court or the Warlocks.

"I'm just curious to know of them, master."

"I understand and so I will tell you of them."

Amzi sighed as they entered the ship and sat down in the seats. The ship's engine roared as it hovered from the ground and flew away with great speed into the sky, disappearing as if it wasn't there.

"The Magus Court is a vast court of wizards and sorcerers. They do not like to be disturbed by outside forces nor bothered with foreign affairs. Their powers are ones to be reckoned with. They take prisoners only for questioning to kill them afterwards. They are confident in their magic and will not hesitate at putting others in their places."

"What of the Warlocks of the West Wind? Their title sounds very similar to what you descried of the Magus Court."

"True, the wizards and warlocks are somewhat one and the same. But, the Warlocks of the West Wind are far different from the Magus Court. They are an elite group of warlocks whom possess the ability to alter the galaxies of the universe to their command if they do so wish. Within their group, there are four elite warlocks who make the decisions regarding all of their plans. They also have younger warlocks to accomplish smaller tasks that do not require to full attention of the elite ones. What gets me about them is their ability to possess both the Avior and the Dekar at once."

"They hold both the light and dark in their hands?"

"Indeed. They are powerful. If they wanted, they could've ended their war with the Keepers and could've taken over the galaxies within an hour."

"Well, why haven't they done it if they have the power to do it?"

"They fear someone of a higher place. His power is vast enough to eliminate them all in the blow of one swoop. An attack from Him could wipe out the entire warlock elite for ever."

"Who's this higher being? I am intrigued to know."

"I can tell you are, Aweran. But, time will give you the answers you are seeking. When the answers do come to you, it will be as if you've already known them. Thanks to the Avior within you."

Amzi nodded as Aweran smiled to him.

"Meanwhile, you and Zeena must prepare your hearts for the confrontation with the Magus Court. I do not know what will await us on Ordow. Be it our answers being answered or our lives being cut short. I do not know."

"I will tell her what you have told me, Master. That way she will not be oblivious to what we may come across in Ordow."

"Do tell her, Aweran and tell her to have faith and let the Avior guide her through the emotions that may cloud her mind given the information that I have given you."

"I will do so, Master."

Aweran returned to his seat in the ship next to Zeena. He tells her of all Amzi has told him regarding the Court, the Warlocks, and the planet of Ordow. Amzi can hear every word that Aweran speaks to Zeena and can feel Zeena staying strong throughout the conversation. From the pilot door walks Evad, who sits next to Amzi.

"So, Ordow, huh."

"Appears to be that way, Evad. You haven't tampered with the Magus Court have you?"

"I've never bothered them with anything. Except maybe a message saying the next time I see one of them, I'm blowing their brains out."

Amzi shook his head and lowered it down. Evad chuckled for a moment.

"Its only a threat, old friend."

"Let's hope they do not have memory of the threat you've given them or else you will be the one who's brains are blown out of your head and it won't be by a range or a blade. But, by their magic which is unseen and unheard."

"You don't have to speak to me like I'm a child, old friend."

"Sometimes I think I do."

"Always the elder you are." Evad said as he left the pilot room, returning to his seat in the corner. Amzi placed the ship on auto pilot and laid back in the chair. He closed his eyes and took in a deep breath.

"High One, let the Avior guide us through this unknown tunnel that we approach. For I know, you will be by our side in any matter."

XVI

THE SORCERY PLANET

The Helio Sor makes its landfall into Ordow, the planet shrouded with a mystical presence. The colors of blue, red, and violet surround the atmosphere of the planet. Aweran looked out of the window at the planet, amazed at its colors and features.

"It looks so beautiful." Aweran said.

"Do not fall into the easy trap of the planet's mystical illusions, Aweran." Amzi said. "That is the first step to falling into their traps. Most men do not even make it pass this first sight."

"Are you saying those colors are an distraction to pull people away from the real matters of the planet?" Zeena said.

"Indeed they are. Keep your mind guarded and your eyes focused for what you are about to witness."

The ship began to enter the atmosphere, drowning in the colors of the planet. Upon surpassing the colors, they noticed the cold, dark ground that awaits them below on the planet. In the distance can be seen a tower. The tower is dark and built with molten rock, layered in magic walls. The Knights gazed at the sight of the tower and noticed smaller towers were sitting aside the tall one. The clouds appeared to be made of shadow, colored in blue as the sky shined red as if lava were flowing above the atmosphere.

"Do we enter the dark tower, Master?" Aweran said.

"I do not think we should." Amzi said. "The Court will

confront us before we find them."

"What happens if we are in a trap and have no way out from the Magus Court?" Evad said. "What of us to do then?"

"We take the fight to them. Be it a necessary precaution against them. Their magic will have to feel our blades. Your range, for you, of course, old friend."

"Where is the location of the star matter, Master?" Orvad said. "Is is somewhere within the dark tower?"

"The Court keeps their items placed in a vault that sits beneath the ground. It would take us to confront their legion of wizards to enter that vault."

"Then we find our way into the vault, master." Novad said. "That way, we can retrieve the star matter and leave this uneasy planet. Its air is soaked in witchcraft."

"That, I can agree with you."

Once the Helio Sor proceeded to land, they stepped out of the ship, looking over the horizon toward the dark tower and the smaller towers. The wind blew through the air, surrounding them as they could feel the magic's power within the air. The scent of the air was that of cinnamon mixed with electricity. The scent entered into their bodies as they could feel the magic becoming stronger with every step they took. Evad kept his hand close to his range as did the Knights with their aduroblades. Aweran held Zeena's hand as they walked toward the towers.

"Don't worry." Aweran said to Zeena. "I will protect you form on here."

"Maybe, I will protect you, young one."

"Funny." Aweran said with a laugh.

Amzi turned toward them. His hand over his mouth, signaling the two to keep themselves quiet. Which they kept quiet.

"This is not the time for such affections, you two." Amzi said. "Keep your focus on why we're here and you will live to see another day."

Evad smirked at Aweran and Zeena. Amzi looked at him, shaking his head.

"Old friend, they are similar to how you behaved during the youth of your days."

"Those times are long gone, Evad." Amzi said. "I am at the age of old now. I have no desire to recite such behaviors as I've done in times past."

"I can see why you wouldn't repeat those acts. But, face it, they're young and they're alive. Its only nature as to what they're doing."

"I am fully aware of such things, Evad. This is not the time to act out those emotions. They can do so when we leave this planet and out of the enemy's hands."

They walked and found themselves at a gate. The gate was made of magic bars, covered in magic aura. Amzi went to touch the gate, but the power of the magic pushed him back, causing him to fall. Aweran ran toward him, helping him up to his feet. Amzi patted Aweran on the shoulder and smiled.

"I haven't felt such a force like that in centuries." Amzi said. "We may have ourselves a battle here."

"How can we fight magic if we can't see it with our own eyes?"

"Trust the Avior to guide you in that matter. For it will show you the arts of your enemies and how to overcome them with the power of the Avior."

"I will hope so."

"Hope you and Zeena shall do. Because from the power that surrounds this gate, we may come across the entire Magus Court."

Amzi commands Orvad to strike toward the gate with his aduroblade. Orvad strikes the gate and its magic slowly weakens. Another strike, the magic continues to weaken. Orvad swiped once more and the gate opened, but not at the hand of Orvad. Amzi knew the Magus Court had been watching them and decided to open the gate themselves, giving them entrance into the magic lands of Ordow.

"It appears they have granted us entrance." Amzi said. "Maybe they demand to seek an audience with us."

"Let's find out, fellas." Evad said. "I'm keeping my hand close to my range. Never know what these mages are up to."

Walking toward the dark tower, which is the command center of the Magus Court, Amzi and the Knights kept guard as they walked through the paths surrounding the smaller towers. Within the smaller towers were wizards and sorcerers in training. Along with some of the minor warlocks. They all kept close by one another as they continued walking up the paths.

"How many do you think live here, Master?" Aweran said.

"Hundreds maybe." Amzi said. "Probably hundreds more than we see with our own eyes."

"Just keep our eyes open as you've said, Master." Zeena said. "We will get pass all of this and collect the star matter."

"That we will accomplish, my lady."

Making their steps closer to the dark tower, they find themselves surrounded in a energy wall made of magic. Amzi and the Knights tried their hardest to break through the wall with their aduroblades, but it proved unsuccessful. They hear footsteps approaching them, looking around and see no one in sight. They turned toward the tower and surrounding them were three wizards of the Magus Court. Cloaked in red and violet robes and hoods, they examined Amzi, the Knights, Aweran, Zeena, and Evad. They spotted their weapons and nodded.

"What are you to make of us, wizards?" Amzi said. "Speak your words now."

"We will take you into our judgment lair, Knights of the Avior." One wizard said. "There, the Court will know of your presence upon our planet."

The wizards teleported themselves along with the Knights into the dark tower. Within a mere second, they were placed inside the judgment lair, surrounded by the entire Magus Court. Amzi looked around and reached for his aduroblade, but it was gone. So was the Knights' aduroblades and Evad's range.

"Those bed timers took my range!" Evad said. "I'm not standing for this kind of shit!"

"You're going to have to deal with it for now, old friend." Amzi said. "Our weapons are in front of their table."

Their weapons laid atop a table near the exit door of the lair. From the door arrived the entire Magus Court, all covered in red and violet robes. They sat around Amzi and the Knights, measuring them and deciphering their attire.

"These robed men are from Helio." A wizard said. "Why are they here on our planet and within our walls?"

"We are here on urgent matters, Magus Court." Amzi said. "If you would just allow us to speak our words, you will have your answers to why you gaze upon us this day."

"Enough words, Abhdi." The Master Wizard said. "You shall speak your words when you are spoken to. You have not been spoken to so far have you."

Amzi stayed quiet as the Court discussed the matters upon themselves, looking at their weapons on the table. The Master Wizard picked up Amzi's aduroblade and measured it. He could sense a power coming from the blade and looked toward him.

"It seems your kind have continued to keep usage of such a weapon. Tell me, what brings you to Ordow and what is your business here and for?"

"We have come here to collect some star matter."

"Why would you need star matter? What are you planning to do with it? What are you aspiring to create with its power?"

"We need the star matter to develop weapons for our

young apprentices. They need them in order to advance to their next stage in becoming Knights of the Covenant."

The Master Wizard looked at Aweran and Zeena. Surprised by the appearance of a female being labeled a apprentice into the Abhdi Knights. He shook his head and pointed toward the two young apprentices.

"Young apprentices you say." The Master Wizard said. "What gives me the notion of a female joining the ranks of the Covenant Knights?"

"The Avior is powerful among her as it is with him." Amzi said. "They will need their weapons to complete their training."

"If the Avior is as powerful as you say within them, how come I only sense its power among you and your three Knights. The Avior truly is powerful amongst the four of you. How come it is not so with these two?"

"They have yet to receive the Avior completely."

"Really? The Avior is powerful amongst them, but they have yet to receive its power completely? How so and why?"

"They have not fully died to themselves to receive the Avior in its complete embodiment."

"What if I were to say that myself and my wizard brothers came up with the decision to kill all of you now and leave your apprentices here to look over your dead bodies? Would they receive the Avior then? Would they fully embrace its power and defeat us in our own planet?"

"Do not listen to his words, both of you." Amzi said. "He is only trying to stir up your emotions to clash at him. If you were to do so, you would open the door for the Dekar to enter into you. That is something I wished not to happen to either of you. Keep your calm and wait patiently for the Avior to come into you."

"When will it come to us, Master?" Aweran said. "I feel as if we are ready to receive it as of right now."

"The High One makes the decision as to who receives it

or not. He will be the final judge in that matter. If He sees it within your hearts to receive the Avior, that He will truly give. As he did to us in our days of youth."

"Are you sure he's telling you both the truth, young apprentices?" The Master Wizard said. "Are you sure he and his Knights are making up false claims to you? To lead you and your lives astray from the real powers of the universe."

"What are the real powers of the universe?" Zeena said.

"Magic, my young ones." The Master Wizard said with a smile. "Sorcery is the true power of the universe!"

"Don't listen to him!" Ebed said. "Keep your minds on the Avior! It will come to you! Trust me!"

"Don't trust him!" The Master Wizard said. "Trust in magic. Trust in the power of sorcery to guide your every step in your lives."

"Young ones!" Novad said. "Listen to Amzi, he's telling you the truth. The Avior will come to you when it is time. Don't give in to the words of this mage."

Evad walked up toward the Master Wizard and raised his hand at him. Smiling toward him. Amzi looked at Evad.

"What are you up to, old friend?"

"I have something in mind." Evad said. "Trust me on this one."

"What do you have to say to me, enashian smuggler?" The Master Wizard said. "What could you possibly say that would make me hinder toward your words? Your words would be only a smear on the ground, waiting for my foot to clear you out."

Evad nodded sarcastically.

"I have a question, Wizard leader." Evad said. "If you could please listen to my words of choice."

"Well then, speak!"

"Ok, ok. I was wondering, since I am not a Knight, nor one of its apprentices, I just figured I could have my range back. If you so please to give it to me."

The Master Wizard commanded one of the wizards to hand him Evad's range pistol. The wizard gave it to the Master, who examined it and grinned facing Evad and holding the pistol.

"This is your weapon of choice, enashian smuggler?!"

"It is. It comes in handy very well. I could show you if you would please let me out of this magic ball of yours."

"Nonsense." The Master Wizard said. "If we were to let you out, you would try to retrieve this primitive weapon and make an attempt at our lives. Nonsense of me to give you release when you aren't even worthy of the word."

Evad turned to Amzi, who looked as if he wanted to punch Evad. Evad shrugged his shoulders.

"Well, I tried something at least."

"Yet you did, old friend." Amzi said. "Now, we must come up with something else besides blowing their brains out."

"Hey, it was a good plan to start with."

"It never was a good plan to begin with, Evad."

The Master Wizard laughed as he looked toward his fellow wizards, who mocked and giggled at the Knights in the magic circle. The Master Wizard quiet the room and looked down at them in the force field of magic.

"What shall we make of them, Magus Court?" The Master Wizard said. "Shall we end their lives as of the others of the past or should we give them what they came here for and let them leave on their way out?"

"Kill them." One half of the Court had spoken.

"Let them live." The other half said. "They will die out there anyhow with the star matter in their possession."

The Master Wizard nodded his head at both side. Deciding amongst them for the final decision. He stood up from his seat, looking down at the Knights below him.

"As of this moment forward, we, the Magus Court, have placed you Knights of the Covenant, your apprentices, and your enashian smuggler to death. Your deaths will be at the hands of the Warlocks of the West Wind."

"No." Zeena said. "This can't be happening right now."

"Have faith, my lady." Amzi said. "The Avior will come to you. Give it some time."

Aweran shook his head as he stared at the Master Wizard. His hands balled up into fists. His anger toward the Wizard clearly showing on his face and his aura was becoming stronger.

"No." Aweran said. "I will slay all of you before you make an attempt at placing any of us to death."

"Is that so, young apprentice of the Knights?" The Master Wizard said. "Very well, show us what kind of power you possess within you."

The ground beneath the lair began to quake as from the opened windows of the lair bolted in a gust of wind. The wind was heavy and it consumed both Aweran and Zeena. Both could feel the wind enter their bodies and embed itself in their hearts and minds. Both began to sit up and stand upright, not making any movement. Their hair blew along with the wind. The wind's power was strong enough to make a crack into the tower's walls and overturned the table where the weapons were placed. Aweran and Zeena both began to speak in an unknown tongue. The speech was difficult for the Master Wizard and his mages to comprehend, but for the Knights it was understanding.

"They're speaking in the Aviorian language, master." Ebed said. "I think they're receiving it."

Amzi looked at both of the apprentices and gazed up to the Master Wizard before placing his eyes back on Aweran and Zeena. He turned to the Knights with a smile on his face.

"They have received the Avior." Amzi said. "They now have the power."

The wind shattered the magic ball and released them from the small space. Aweran and Zeena looked at each other. Smiling with energy and they nodded to Amzi and the Knights.

Evad looked on with a slight concern for his life at the moment.

"The hell is going on?" Evad said. "I wasn't built for this kind of stuff."

The Master Wizard stood up from his seat as the other wizards began to leave the room in fear. Afraid of what gave them the Avior. Though, the Master Wizard stood tall, facing them all.

"What power I sense from the two of you." He said. "The power is strong and it is bound to your spirits. What is that?"

"It is the Avior." Aweran said. "Now, we have control over its power. To do with it as we are given to do so."

The aduroblades returned to the Knights and so did Evad's range. They grabbed their weapons and entered combat with the wizards. Magic fighting against advanced tech. Evad blasted his range toward the Master Wizard, who deflected the energy beams toward the wall.

"You really believe such a weapon would harm a powerful figure such as myself?!" He said. "Enashians are really ignorant in their own devices."

"At least I tried taking you out, old timer."

The Master Wizard fired magic lighting toward Evad, who dodged it by running and ducking beneath the seats of the Court. While the fighting was taking place, a blast of light flashes into the judgment lair, ceasing all the fighting. Everyone took a look to see where the light had come from and standing in the middle of the lair was an old man, with long gray hair, who wore a worn out dark gray robe and a white cloak. He removed his hood and it was revealed to be Gaulhan the Wizard, a legendary figure who is said to live on the outskirts of Ordow, away from the Magus Court and Warlocks.

"What brings you hear, Old Mage?!" The Master Wizard said.

"I have come to cease this conflict and grant these

individual a safe passage back to their ship so they may leave."

"We're not leaving without the star matter." Aweran said. "Where is it located?"

Gaulhan reached into his robe and pulled out the star matter. The matter was glowing brightly, a blue and white aura. As if smaller stars were connected to the matter. He handed it to Amzi who placed it inside his robe pocket.

"Now, leave." Gaulhan said. "Make sure to never return here unless you want to see your lives ended abruptly."

"I will not let them leave this place with that matter alive!" The Master Wizard said.

"That you will do." Gaulhan said, raising up his staff and pointing it toward the Master Wizard, blasting him with a magic energy, causing him to fly out of the window toward the ground beneath.

"Is he dead?" Aweran said, looking out to the Master Wizard's fallen body.

"He lives, young man." Gaulhan said. "But, he is unconscious for the moment. Now, for your sakes, leave this place."

They exited the judgment lair and walked back to the outside where they could see the Master Wizard laying on the ground, unconscious from the fall. walking behind them is Gaulhan, who guides them back to their ship.

"Keep yourselves safe and keep that star matter protected." Gaulhan said. "Be it well with you, Knights."

"We will keep this matter in safe keepings." Amzi said. "Trust in us."

"I will trust in your actions, Abhdi Knight. Not the words you speak toward me."

Amzi nodded. Showing respect to Gaulhan.

"Fair enough."

They entered the ship and prepared for takeoff. The Helio Sor hovered and flew away as Gaulhan watched it disappear into the sky. Gaulhan turned back toward the tower and vanished into thin air.

XVII

THE FINAL PHASE

The Knights make their return to Dagobar. The Orchs of the Grogok Clan were awaiting their return as King Krak stood outside of his castle, watching the Helio Sor make its landing into their area. He could sense a interstellar energy coming from the ship as they proceeded to exit.

"Do you think they have the star matter, my lord?" A Orch soldier said.

"Let us see and find out." Krak said.

Amzi and the Knights approached Krak with the orchs surrounding them once again. Krak looked at Aweran and Zeena, he could sense an energy flowing from their bodies.

"What has become of your two young ones, Knight?"

"They have received the Avior since they believed." Amzi said. "They are now ready for the bigger obstacles in this life."

Krak nodded with respect toward the two. He invited them back into the blacksmith area of the Grogok Castle. Within the area, the blacksmith orchs were prepared to manufacture the weapons Amzi had spoken about. Krak turned toward him with his hand extended out in front.

"The star matter, Knight."

"Right you are, King Krak." Amzi said, handing the star matter to Krak. Krak analyzed the star matter and nodded gently before handing it to his blacksmiths.

"Build the weapons of the Knights." Krak said. "Do it

with as much haste as you can conjure up."

"We have time to wait until they are completed of course." Amzi said. "We are not in such a hurry."

"You're sure about that, old friend?" Evad said. "Because I don't feel quite comfortable standing around a bunch a brutish orchs and standing inside their domain makes me feel naked."

"You'll get over it, Evad. Make sure of that."

They waited and waited as the blacksmiths developed the weapons and coated them with the star matter. After about two and a half hours, the blacksmiths walked out of the room to Amzi and the Knights standing in the throne room of Krak. The blacksmiths handed the weapons to Amzi and returned to their room.

"Your weapons are completed, Knight." Krak said. "How do they feel to your liking?"

Amzi examined the weapons and smiled before handing them each to Aweran and Zeena. They grabbed the weapons and stated at Amzi with a slight lost of words.

"These are for us, Master?" Aweran said, glancing at the weapon in his hands. "Seriously?"

"You have received the Avior within you. With that, you are now able to possess an aduroblade of your own. Hence forth, the two of you are now a part of *Those of the Avior*."

Aweran raised up his aduroblade, which was coated in a dark blue energy as the sword appeared to be made of orch metal and energy. Zeena's aduroblade was in fact an adurostaff, which both ends of the staff were coated in a bright green and was made of almost all energy with minor details of steel. They celebrated their elevated status of becoming true Abhdi Knights and Knights of the Ancient Covenant. Krak applauded them, walking down the steps of his throne.

"I see you are happy with your weapons." Krak said.

"Truly, your clan is the best at the art of blacksmith, King Krak." Amzi said. "I thank you for your service in helping us."

"Better of you to choose our aid rather than the aid of the dwarves in Sudravor. Sometimes they can be costly."

"As I have once known."

Amzi and the Knights were ready to leave as Krak escorted them back to the outside. While making their steps toward the outside of the castle, shouts and screams could be heard coming from around the Grogok landscape. They all ran quickly to see what was taking place and right in front of them, in their land was the rival orch clan called the Tukoeater Clan, lead by their leader Sodang Brok. Brok walked with a strut as the skull necklaces and bracelets upon his body rocked along with each footstep he took. Krak roared toward him, holding up his war sword and prepared for combat. Sodang chuckled as behind him approached Dos and her army of howlshockers.

"Dos has found us." Orvad said. "She has come to our location unaware, master."

"It seems she has forsaken the rainshockers and has been give usage of the howlshockers." Novad said.

Sodang turned to Dos, who stood beside him. Both shook hands as they gazed the landscape of the Grogok Clan.

"It appears you are outwitted, Krak!" Sodang said. "Perhaps, you could prove yourself wise to best me in battle."

"I will tear your head from your shoulders and make the ground drink your blood!"

"So be it."

Sodang roared with his warhammer held high above his head, leading his clan into war with the Grogok Clan. Behind them run the howlshockers, being commanded by Dos, who ran beside them, yelling as she swung around her adurowhip. Krak and his army of orchs were prepared for the fight. Amzi approached Krak, holding his aduroblade in his hand.

"We will fight with you, King Krak." Amzi said. "It is the best that we can do for you after what you've done for us."

Krak nodded.

"Together we fight, Knights. Together we will win."

The Grogok army was set as was Amzi and the Knights. Aweran and Zeena were also prepared for the fight coming their way. They stood still, concentrating the Avior into the battlefield. The sounds of roars and shouts were coming closer and growing louder by every second that passed them by. The rival clan and the howlshockers were coming much closer, the intensity that filled the battlefield was as powerful as the ray's of the sun burning through the ground.

"NOW!" Sodang roared.

"SLAUGHTER THEM ALL!" Krak yelled.

The Grogok and Tukoeater clans collided with each other with the force of a mountain ramming into another mountain. Instead both mountains would have cracks growing within them. The armies of both sides smashed each other with their swords and hammers. Others decided to use their fists and teeth to bleed out the opposing clan. Dos and the howlshockers faced down the Knights and Evad. She smiled toward them and noticed the energy soaring from Aweran and Zeena.

"What have they become?" Dos said. "The energy I sense from them is strange and unusually powerful."

"They are Knights of the Covenant." Amzi said. "Like myself and my brothers in arms."

"That makes it much more better to see two more of you that will meet your ends at the slash of my adurowhip."

Dos commands the howlshockers to attack the Knights and their battle begins with the aduroblades colliding with the energy shields and batons of the howlshockers. Aweran and Zeena surround Dos, who smiles at them both, slashing her adurowhip into the ground, causing a tiny tremor, knocking the both of them off their feet.

"Your newfound power will not save your lives from me." Dos said.

"We will overcome you with our newfound power and

you will be the one to fall on this day." Aweran said.

"What he said is true and will come to pass." Zeena said. "Are you ready to meet your end, huntress?"

"Better to worry of your own end rather then the end of mine."

Aweran and Zeena swung their aduroblades to Dos, who grabbed them with the adurowhip and kicked Aweran to the ground. Swinging blows with Zeena until she knees Zeena in the abdomen and tosses her into one of the nearby hovels. Dos smirked, wiping her face from the flying dirt in the air from the battles of the orch clans. Zeena looked up toward Dos, who taunted her arrogantly.

"Stand up, Dame of the Covenant!" Dos said. "Face me like a woman!"

Zeena yelled as she rammed into Dos with her adurostaff and they battled with twists and turns. Aweran went for a slash to Dos, which she jumped over and kicked Aweran in the jaw with the front of her boot. Dos laughed as she blocked the attacks from Zeena's adurostaff.

"They call you Knights?! A fable worth telling the Viper Order."

"You make a joke of us, huntress." Zeena said. "Wait till the universe hears the tale of your defeat at the hands of two novice Knights."

Trees began to crash and fall to the ground while the civil war of the orch clans continued to take place. Krak and Sodang clashing their swords and hammers together with anger flowing through their eyes. Krak kicked Sodang in his knee and jammed his own knee into Sodang's jaw.

"Appears you are weakening, Sodang!" Krak said.

"I am not dead yet, Grodak!" Sodang said. "Now, face me like you mean it or you will see the downfall of your feeble clan!"

Krak roared, slamming his sword against Sodang's hammer continually. The Knights had near defeated most of the howlshockers, except for three who were highly trained in the art of aduroblade combat. An orch from the Tukoeater clan ran toward the Knights. Ebed swiped the orch in its stomach with his aduroblade, cutting the beast in half. Evad had climbed the castle and took shots down at the battling orchs. Firing his range and blasting orchs in their shoulders, heads, and legs. Evad savored the moment of taking the shots. Laughing as he pulled the trigger.

"I love this kind of shit!"

Evad fired more range blasts until he spotted an orch standing afar off with a cannon. Which he fired and the cannon blasted the wall of the castle where Evad was standing. He ran down the corridor from the falling ground. Evad jumped and grabbed onto the opposite wall as the wall he was once leaning against was falling to the ground in rubble.

"Sure hope no one was standing there."

The land was covered in orch corpses across every corner near the Grogok Castle. Krak and Sodang continued their bout as both leaders were become tired and their stamina was declining. The Knights had finished off the remainder of the howlshockers, which caught Dos' attention as she turned back to face Aweran and Zeena. They stared at her and jolted their hands toward her, giving off an Avior blast, which slammed Dos into one of the hovels, bursting her through its wooden walls. Aweran and Zeena looked at one another as Dos slowly walked out of the crashed hovel, holding her right arm.

"What in the hell was that?!" Dos said. "What kind of power have the both of you consumed?!"

"That was the power of the Avior you have felt, huntress." Aweran said. "Would you like another touch of its power?"

"This war is not yet over." Dos said running back to her ship. Zeena went to chase her, but Aweran held her back.

"She's getting away, Aweran!"

"You'll have another time to stop her." Aweran said.

"Trust me. You'll be seeing her again in no time."

The orch armies were all but finished. Not a single orch soldier was standing except for their leader who began to fight near the castle walls. Aweran and Zeena went to aid Krak, but Amzi stopped them.

"King Krak can deal with his rival himself." Amzi said. "His strength has not yet been revealed to us."

Krak swiped his sword at Sodang's hammer, which clashed once more together. Sodang went for a punch and Krak caught his arm, cutting it off with his sword. Sodang roared in pain as he dropped his hammer and fell to his knees. Krak took his sword and impaled Sodang in his chest. Sodang's breath was begging to cease as Krak walked behind Sodang and held his head in between his hands.

"This war between us is over, Sodang!" Krak said, tearing the head of Sodang off from his shoulders. Roaring in victory, holding Sodang's head above him as the blood dripped onto his chest.

The sound of ship had sounded and gathered everyone's attention. The ship was of Dos who was flying away from the land and exiting the planet. Zeena watched as Dos' ship disappeared into the sky.

"Another time, huntress." Zeena said.

Krak approached the Knights with the severed head of Sodang. The Knights nodded to him as they looked around at the decimation of the land. Hovels destroyed, hundreds dead from both sides and the castle wall destroyed.

"Appears that the remainder of my clan have much work to do."

"It is so." Amzi said. "We can help you."

"You've helped me enough, Knight." Krak said. "I thank you for the assistance in ending this civil war."

"The pleasure is ours, King Krak."

From the castle walked out Evad, who stared at the Knights and gestured toward Amzi the wall falling and himself latching onto the edge. Evad approached Krak and patted him on the shoulder.

"Sorry about your wall, your highness." Evad said. "Though, I did what I could to stop the orch who fired the cannon."

"So you say, enash."

Evad walks up to Amzi, looking around at the destruction of the land.

"So, can we go now?"

"Yeah. We can go."

The Knights approached their ship and entered it. Upon preparing for takeoff, the ship's message holder began to beep constantly. Amzi looked at it, uncertain of what is going on with the machine. He pressed the button and arose a red hologram. The hologram was an image of both Sinth Cain and Sinth Kara. Standing on the grounds of a planet.

"Knights of the Ancient Covenant of Elyon." Sinth Cain said. "I have grown tired of chasing you down throughout the sectors of the universe. I have decided through my own power and will, to send you this message of combat. Let us end this thousand age war between us once and for all. Meet myself, my wife, and my army on the planet of Thran. Come and face us, Knights. Protect your unworthy covenant or come to meet your end and watch as the Viper Order grows and consumes all of the universe."

"We await you all." Sinth Kara said. "I hope you can come and greet us. Please, we insist."

The hologram had shut down and the Knights looked at one another. Evad took off his hat and wiped his forehead and exhaled.

"Thran, huh?" Evad said. "That planet of destruction?"

"What do you say of the challenge, Master?" Ebed said. "They want us to go to Thran to meet our deaths."

"Thran is inhabited with destruction and war." Novad said. "It is the primary place to resolve this conflict between us and them."

"We can finally be rid of this Viper Order once and for all, master." Orvad said. "Finish what our ancestors could not."

Amzi looked at Aweran and Zeena. He walked toward them and hugged them both. Not knowing how to response to such an action. They hugged him back.

"What do the two of you suggest we do?" Amzi said. "Shall we proceed to Thran and end the Viper Order for good or shall we decline their offer and have them to continue to chase us down across the universe?"

Aweran and Zeena glanced at each other before facing Amzi. They nodded to him and toward the other Knights.

"I suggest we go to Thran." Aweran said. "End this war once and for all."

"I agree with Aweran all the way." Zeena said. "Let's go to Thran, Master."

Amzi nodded as he walked back to the pilot seat. The ship takes off and travels into space. Amzi turned back to the Knights sitting amongst each other and smiled.

"To Thran we go." Amzi said. "Aviorspeed."

Across the sectors, the Viper Order had already made their way toward Thran and have landed on the war-torn planet during the warfare on Dagobar. The clouds of Thran are dark and gray as thunder clapped its way across the sky. The ground red and glowing as magma. Walking out of the Viper ship called the Sinth-Tred is both Sinth Cain and Sinth Kara. They turn around to see the massive ship called the Attonbitus arrive and within it are thousands of rainshockers and Imperial Viper Knights, who are dressed in black and red robes with their red aduroblades out. Waiting for the Knights' decision to make itself known.

"Do you think they'll come, my love?" Sinth Kara said.

"For their sake, I hope they never make it here. If they happen to arrive, we know what to do with them."

XVIII

BATTLE OF THRAN

Sinth Cain and Sinth Kara stand on the grounds of Thran, facing the sky, awaiting the arrival of the Knights of the Covenant. The rainshockers surround the perimeter of the selected battlefield with the Imperial Viper Knights keeping a close distance around the Viper Lords. The area was quiet, except for the occasional thunder claps that would come from the dark clouds above.

"Maybe they won't show themselves at all." Sinth Kara said. "I believe they fear us and they fear the power of the Dekar. What it can do to them as opposed to their Avior power."

"I have told you not to speak so low concerning the Avior, Kara. You do not know its true power."

"I don't think you fully understand what you even possess, my Cain. We possess the power of the Dekar. We are stronger than Those of the Avior and their High One. We are the true dominators of the universe. We are true power."

The clouds clapped with a louder thunder, getting the attention of both Cain and Kara as the Helio Sor makes it way through the clouds, covered in lightning and landing on the red grounds of Thran. The rainshockers raised up their plasma ranges toward the ship and the Viper Knights stood their grounds, holding their aduroblades steady.

"They are arrived." Cain said. "Prepare yourself, Kara. It is a war that we are about to engage in."

Within the Helio Sor, Amzi talks with the Knights and Evad about what is to come upon the battlefield of Thran. They join hands and gather together in a prayer. Silencing themselves within. Amzi speaks to the High One, to let the Avior flow through them all in order to gain the victory against the Viper Order. They release their hands as the ship's door opened. They walked out, seeing the Viper Lords and their army standing before them.

"The Knights have answered our calling." Cain said.

"We are here as you asked, Sinth Cain." Amzi said. "What have you to say now?"

"What do I have to say? I say, we end this conflict between our forces. Finally bringing peace into the universe for the generations coming behind us."

Amzi measured Cain's words. Noticing a strange conflict taking place within Cain's own being.

"You talk as if you're a different breed of Viper Lord. What has become of you? Something has transpired in your spirit."

Kara turned to Cain and glared toward Amzi. Her eyes fired up with rage toward the Knights. Her pupils began to glow red as she raised up her own aduroblade and yells at them with a loud scream.

"We destroy these feeble Knights once and for all!" Kara said. "We make sure the Dekar rules the universe for ever!"

Throughout the sky appeared a variety of Eglahs, the round and pointed starfighter ships of the Viper Order. Kara gazed up toward them and smiled, showing the Knights her smile. Amzi nodded and point up above them. Kara looked around them as did Cain.

"We did not come alone."

From above the Knights came down the Emerald Cavalier Force, wearing their green and black uniforms and shaded in their glowing green aura along with the Revolter Squadron, flying down with their Aver-Wings, Xathos-Wings, and Yavos-Wings. Being lead by their captain in the Ark-Celeritas, the leading starfighter of them all.

"You have your fighters of the air." Amzi said. "As do we."

"Enough of this nonsense!" Kara said. "My love, let's take the battle to them. Kill them all and end this period!"

"As we shall, my queen." Cain said.

Cain turned toward the rainshockers and the Viper Knights. He raised up both the Sinthblade and his aduroblade in the air and pointed them toward the Knights.

"Wipe them out." Cain said. "All of them."

The rainshockers ran toward the Knights as did the Viper Knights, who lead the way into battle. Cain and Kara walked behind the rainshockers, their weapons prepared for battle. Amzi turned to Aweran and Zeena. Each of the Knights have their aduroblades out and ready. Evad stood steady with his range in hand.

"This is gonna get ugly." Evad said. "But, I like ugly."

"Are you both ready for this?" Amzi said.

"We are, Master." Aweran said. "We both are ready."

Amzi nodded and raised up his aduroblade.

"For the High One!" Amzi said.

The Knights ran toward the Viper Knights with the rainshockers behind. The Eglahs flew in the air toward the Emerald Cavaliers and Revolter Squadron. The battle began on the ground with the Knights clashing aduroblades with the Viper Knights. Evad fires toward the rainshockers, hitting them in their heads and chests. Amzi and the three Knights battled the Viper Knights on their own. Aweran and Zeena both stood, swiping at the incoming rainshockers, looking pas them toward Cain and Kara.

"It seems the two want us." Kara said. "Shall we give us over?"

"We shall." Cain said.

Aweran and Cain ran toward each other as did Zeena

and Kara. Both sides engaged in aduroblade combat with Aweran having to use the Avior to guide him in facing Cain with both the Sinthblade and aduroblade. Kara swung her aduroblade, colliding with Zeena's adurostaff. Zeena kicks Kara in her leg and punches her.

"What strong feats you have, little Zeena."

"I've waited for this moment a long time." Zeena said. "You kept me locked away in that prison on false charges."

"It was the only way to get you away from the truth and grow further to the lie."

"Your attempt didn't work. I've come much closer to the truth thanks to you."

"How dare you."

Both clashed their aduroblade and adurostaff. The energy coming off the blades was strong enough that it started to burn the air around them. Aweran continued to swing around his aduroblade against Cain's Sinthblade and aduroblade. Cain laughed as the two were in combat.

"I feel the Avior within you, boy!"

"It gives me the strength to end your reign of destruction."

"My reign will live on through the power of the Dekar!"

The ships of both sides continued to battle in the air. Blasting energy beams into the opposing ships, crashing them down to the Thran grounds. From the air, comes down another ship, the ship of Dos. She witnesses the sky battle as well as the ground battle. She lands her ship and jumps out of it, running toward Zeena and Kara with her adurowhip in hand. Twirling the adurostaff toward Kara, Zeena turns and is speared by Dos, who holds her to the ground. Going for a series of punches which Zeena dodges every one of them and blasts Dos off of her with the Avior power. Kara goes for a stab, but is stopped by Zeena's adurostaff.

"It won't be that easy."

Aweran and Cain continued their fierce battle. Swiping

the aduroblades against each other, giving off sparks of energy. Falling to the ground and burning it within seconds. Aweran kicked Cain and swiped the Sinthblade from Cain's right hand.

"One blade down." Aweran said. "One more to go."

"You think I can't take you with just the aduroblade. You are surely mistaken. I am a Viper Lord for a reason."

Both clashing their aduroblades against each other. Having out a test of strengths, trying to shove the other back and onto the ground. Cain laughs throughout the entire bout. The dog fights in the air between the Squadron and the Eglahs continue with their captain giving commands to attack the Attonbitus, which is the command center for the Eglahs. Vulture Drone come flying out of the Attonbitus and toward the starfighters, crashing into them without notice.

"Change of plans!" The Captain said. "Fire your energy toward the Vulture Drones. They are suicidal drones!"

Members of the Emerald Cavalier Force fly toward the Vulture Drones, grabbing them by their heads and ripping them apart before taking out other Eglahs around them. One Eglah swoops past an Emerald Cavalier, puling off the medallion from his neck, suddenly falling to the ground before being caught by another Emerald Cavalier.

"Not yet."

The Cavalier retrieved the other's medallion. Handing it back to him as he placed it own, gaining back his Emerald powers. Flying towards the Eglah which swooped by. On the ground, the rainshockers were dying from the crashing ships and firing shots from Evad. Some died from making an attempt toward the Knights who have nearly defeated the Viper Knights except for a few.

"There's only three more of them, master." Ebed said.

"We take them out." Amzi said. "Get rid of them completely."

The Knights battled the Imperial Viper Knights, clashing aduroblades and fighting with their legs and arms to finish them off. Zeena swung her adurostaff against both Kara and Dos who decided to team up against her. Zeena twirted the adurostaff, knicking Kara to the ground with the Avior blast and impaling Dos with the adurostaff. Dos fell to her knees, dropping her adurowhip.

"I told you." Zeena said.

Dos fell to the grounds of Thran and died. Zeena and Kara continued to battle each other. Both becoming tired. Aweran and Cain were slowly becoming worn out, clashing their aduroblades constantly and trying to gain oxygen in their surroundings as the blades were consuming the air around them.

"I can feel you wearing out, boy." Cain said. "I have the advantage of this battle now!"

"I think not." Aweran said. "I still have the power of the Avior to aid me."

Cain swung his aduroblade, knocking the blade out of Aweran's hand and raised up his left hand, attacking him with the Dekar Lightning. The red lightning, glowing darkly and quickly consuming Aweran as he screams out in pain. Falling to his knees.

"They didn't teach you the difference of feats between the Avior and the Dekar did they, boy?!"

Aweran tries to fight back, but is unable to retrieve his aduroblade laying on the ground. Cain laughed as he continued blasting him with the Dekar Lightning. Aweran laud still on the ground as Cain raised up his aduroblade above Aweran.

"Now, you will understand the true power of Those of the Dekar!"

Cain went for a slash, but Aweran moved out of the way as the ground began to quake. Everyone on the ground had ceased fighting. Feeling the strength of the quake becoming stronger and they happen to notice they were fighting near a volcano. The volcano began to shake. The volcano had a release of magma come down and the center had burst open. The magma from the volcano flowed throughout the battlefield and entered into the sea of Thran that laid nearby the ships. With the magma entering the sea, the waters began to boil and from the waters sounded off a roar. Everyone turned to the waters and from them arose the Thran Beast. A large dragon that lived beneath the sea.

The Thran Beast, thought to be only of myth had risen out of the sea. Its scales colored in black and red and its eyes appeared as if they were fire surging within them. Its loud roar ceased the thunder in the clouds as it flew out of the sea and toward the battlefield. Exhaling streams of fire from its mouth toward the ground. Burning the remaining rainshockers. Remnants of the fire had slightly touched both Aweran and Cain, burning their uniforms and flesh.

The Thran Beast flew into the air and entered the dog fights between the ships with its wings knocking both the Eglahs and Vulture Drones to the ground. The Ark-Celeritas flew past the Thran Beast, almost colliding into its side. The captain shook his head.

"What the hell was that thing?!"

Amzi and the Knights watched the Thran Beast fly through the air, destroying ships in its path.

"I thought the creature had died out centuries ago." Novad said.

"Appears that it lives and it is angry." Amzi said. "Let us finish what we've come for."

Kara was stuck between some debris from the crashed Eglahs. Zeena approached her and went to kill her, but stopped herself. Kara became angry as Zeena's ceasing. Shaking the debris around her.

"You better kill me!" Kara said with a sinister laugh. "You better kill me, Zeena!"

"No. I won't do it. I won't become what you've already made yourself into."

"You petite fool!"

Zeena walked away as Kara continued to yell at each. Screaming for her to kill her. Aweran and Cain continued the battle, even after being weakened by the fire of The Thran Beast. Cain quickly went for a swing, but Aweran raised up his palm, stopping Cain's swing with the Avior and retrieved his aduroblade from the ground to the side. Aweran held his aduroblade and swiped it against Cain's chest. Cain stood frozen as he stared at Aweran. He turned, facing Kara, who could sense his life flowing out of him.

"NO!" Kara yelled.

Cain fell to the ground, presumably died as his chest slowly was opened in half. Kara screamed as she blasted the Eglah debris from around her and ran toward Aweran with her aduroblade.

"You will pay for this!" Kara said.

She ran toward Aweran and tripped her foot on a rock and fell into a sharp metal that was once a Vulture Drone. Kara's head fell against the drone debris, to which she had knocked herself out instantly from the impact. Aweran gave off a sign of relief and as he went to turn to Zeena, a shadow figure manifested before him. Only he could see the figure, which was shrouded in shadow. A fog of smoke, difficult to see through.

"Who are you?" Aweran said.

"You. You!." The shadow said. "The Avior has made you powerful. But, I sense something else within you. The Dekar."

"The Dekar doesn't have a place within me. Only the Avior does."

"Not as of this moment. The Avior yet lives within you, but your aggression, your focus is giving in to the Dekar. In time, you will learn to receive it and use it along with the Avior. Both powers of light and dark, within your grasp. Seize it, Aweran and you will become more powerful than anyone you've known. Even the Knights and even Amzi Grake.

Imagine the power you could possess within your hands. Within your mind. Within your spirit.."

"I won't listen to this."

'You won't as of this moment. But in time, you will know that I am right."

"Who are you?!"

"I am a friend. A close friend. We will meet soon. Very soon."

The shadow evaporated as Amzi and the Knights approached him. Seeing Aweran startled a bit. Amzi placed his hand on Aweran's shoulder and smiled.

"The battle is over." Amzi said. "We have one."

"Seems we have, Master." Aweran said with a faint smile.

Evad walked up to Aweran and shook his hand.

"Didn't know you could handle yourself so well."

"The Avior lead me through."

"Nah! You did it!"

"No, Evad. The Avior lead me through the battle. Without it, I would've died."

"If you say so, kid."

The Ark-Celeritas landed as the captain approached Amzi and the two shook hands.

"We've won, Captain."

"We have." The Captain said. "Anytime you need our assistance, we will be there."

"I will count on it."

The Revolter Squadron and Emerald Cavaliers left the planet as did the Knights. Later, a ship landed on Thran, with a hooded figure walking through the battlefield, seeing the dead bodies of those that fell and approaches the body of the presumed dead Sinth Cain and the unconscious Sinth Kara. The hooded figure reaches down and picked up both the Sinthblade and their aduroblades. His crew of imperial rainshockers picked up Cain and Kara, returning them to his ship which flies out of Thran with the Thran Beast looking out at the horizon within the seas. Snarling as it sucked its head beneath the dark waters.

    A short period of time after the battle of Thran, the Knights made their return to Helio in the city of Tropolton. The city restored with its people and Aweran and Zeena being made official Knights of the Covenant. With the inclusion of Aweran and Zeena, Amzi names them all Knights of the Advanced Covenant. Outside of the temple, Aweran and Zeena stood together, holding hands and kissing as the Helio sun set before them.

    Amzi walks out of the temple and notices the two and smiles. Ebed walks up behind him, looking at the two young Knights standing together. Happiness flowing from within their being.

    "So, this is the restoration of all things that was spoken of?" Ebed said.

    "No, Ebed." Amzi said. "This is a new beginning of things to come.

THE SAGA CONTINUES IN:

EverWar
UNIVERSE
THE DAMNED ONES

ABOUT THE AUTHOR

Ty'Ron W. C. Robinson II is the author of several works of fiction. Including the *Dark Titan Universe Saga* series (*Dark Titan Knights, The Resistance Protocol, Tales of the Scattered, Tales of the Numinous, Day of Octagon*), *The Haunted City Saga* series, and the *Symbolum Venatores* series.

Also of other books (*Lost in Shadows, The Book of The Elect, etc.*) and One-Shot short stories.

More information pertaining to the author and stories can be found at darktitanentertainment.com.

Twitter: @TyRonRobinsonII

Twitter: @DarkTitan_
Instagram: @darktitanentertainment
Facebook: @DarkTitanEnt
Pinterest: @darktitanentertainment
YouTube: Dark Titan Entertainment

www.ingramcontent.com/pod-product-compliance
Lightning Source LLC
LaVergne TN
LVHW041855070526
838199LV00045BB/1609